A WIFE IN EVERY SENSE

EUROPE'S HOTTEST BILLIONAIRES

JOANNE WALSH

Entangled Publishing, LLC
2614 South Timberline Road
Suite 109
Fort Collins, CO 80525
Visit our website at www.entangledpublishing.com.

Indulgence is an imprint of Entangled Publishing, LLC.

Edited by Liz Pelletier
Cover design by Kelley York
Cover art from Shutterstock

Manufactured in the United States of America

First Edition September 2015

Prologue

"It meant nothing, Kate. It was just a game…a bit of fun."

She stood frozen to the spot with shock in the middle of the saloon bar of the Boar's Head, a quaint old-world pub in the heart of England. It was a favorite student haunt, and to-night—Saturday—it was full to bursting with revelers from Camford's famous, ancient, top-flight university. She was dimly aware that a circle of onlookers had formed around her and Oliver—just like the spectators who, two hundred years ago, would have watched the cockfights reputed to have taken place in this wood-paneled, low-beamed room.

Oliver Temperley-Smythe stood tall and stony faced, his handsome, aristocratic features showing no emotion or kindness as he repeated, "It was a game…a bit of fun."

Kate felt as though she'd been stabbed through the heart.

"I don't understand," she pleaded. "You said you loved me."

Oliver shrugged. "Yeah, well, it was what you wanted to hear…and"—a satisfied smile played around his lips—"I won the bet."

The watching crowd had gone very quiet now, and within its ranks somebody sniggered.

A storm of hurt and disbelief whirled in Kate's brain, and for a moment she thought her knees were going to give way, but she willed herself to stay standing.

"A *bet*," she echoed. "You went out with me for three months, convinced me that you loved me and slept with me for a *bet*?"

Oliver's expression took on a haughty sneer. "Yeah. The Bucks had a wager going this semester. Members had to find first years. *Virgins.*" He wore a triumphant smile when he uttered that last word. "You were the only one who came across."

"But Ollie, I thought we had a relationship," Kate persisted, tears trickling now, causing her mascara to make inky trails under her eyes and on her cheeks. "I believed what you told me. That you cared about me."

"Sorry. Look, I don't know why you're getting so upset. We had a good time, didn't we? And you got broken in into the bargain."

"*Broken in?* I'm not a horse!" Kate's fists clenched with indignation.

One of Oliver's fellow Bucks moved out of the crowd and tapped his arm. "C'mon, mate, leave her. She's just another slag. We're going on to the Red Lion."

Oliver stood for a moment and surveyed Kate and her smeary, distraught face, then he turned to leave without another word. The show finished, the onlookers nudged and pushed past Kate as she remained standing like a statue, trying to take in what had just happened to her.

She's just another slag. The cruel, cold words bit at her like frostbite, deep enough to scar.

Chapter One

"We could talk about it over dinner this evening…"

The blonde sitting opposite Aleksei Aleksanou leaned forward as she breathed her suggestion. If he read the invitation in Denise Ferguson's heavily made-up eyes correctly, she was hoping they could seal the deal later in his bed. But he was not interested. For a start, there was no need; they'd already reached an agreement without having to mix business with pleasure. And anyway, he had more important matters to attend to.

"That would have been very pleasant, but I'm already otherwise engaged."

"What a shame," she pouted. She sat back and flicked her bleached, streaked hair extensions over her shoulder, her sharp eyes roaming hungrily over his muscular physique. "Got a hot date?"

Aleksei smiled and shook his head. "I'm taking my personal assistant to dinner. Kate's leaving at the end of the week to go traveling, and I want to show my appreciation to her and thank her for all that's she done for me."

Denise's penciled eyebrow shot up. "*Appreciation?*" She dragged out the word suggestively. "She's a *very* lucky girl."

Aleksei waved a conversational hand, deliberately misunderstanding the innuendo behind Denise's words. "No, I'm the lucky one. Or maybe unlucky. Kate's been a gem—she's going to be a real loss to my team." He needed to turn the conversation back to business. "Okay, we have a deal. I will arrange for the contracts to be sent to you as soon as possible for your signature." He stood up, signaling that the meeting was over.

"**P**ut me through to Aleksei—now!"

Kate tried her hardest not to bridle at the demanding female voice and replied as calmly as she could, "Miss Jones, as I explained to you, Mr. Aleksanou is in a meeting. But if you would like me to take a message for you, I will make sure he gets it as soon as he is free."

"I know he's there!" The already shrill tones of supermodel Phoenix Jones raised another notch. "And I know you're stonewalling me! You didn't pass on my message after I called yesterday."

Kate swallowed down a sigh. She had given her Greek boss Phoenix's message yesterday afternoon, but clearly Aleksei had chosen not to return the call. Kate knew the score: Aleksei's affair with Phoenix had run its course, but she was finding it hard to accept. No doubt the supermodel would shortly be the recipient of a beautiful gift of an exquisite necklace and matching earrings from one of London's most upmarket jewelers. Kate knew just how gorgeous the good-bye gifts he gave were — she'd ordered a number of sets for his cast-off women during her time as his PA.

Right now, Phoenix was being treated to the same discreet silence that Aleksei always employed when he decided his relationships were over. He was not a man to involve himself in messy emotional situations. And from what Kate had observed of the tall, lithe, impossibly lovely-looking brunette, when her farewell of fabulous bling arrived, no doubt Phoenix's anger would disappear quicker than a champagne cocktail.

"Miss Jones," Kate responded, her voice pleasant but firm, "Mr. Aleksanou is very, very busy at the moment. He already has yesterday's message, and I will be certain to tell him that you called again today."

"You'd better, you stuck-up little cow. Well, one thing's for sure — you won't be blocking me next time I call. I hear that he's ditched you."

If only she could tell Phoenix Jones that, actually, she'd handed in her notice, but she held her tongue. "Thank you, Miss Jones. I've made a note of everything you've had to say and I'll make sure Mr. Aleksanou receives it."

She replaced the handset firmly in its cradle and got up, taking the message slip into Aleksei's office and placing it on his desk. It was strange to think that after Friday she'd no longer be in these familiar surroundings. She glanced around the room, her attention drawn again to the huge oil painting that depicted a sunlit Greek bay surrounded by creamy yellow sandstone cliffs and dark green pines. The focal point of the painting was a small rock island in the middle of the aquamarine sea, on which stood a small classical six-columned marble temple.

The painting had always intrigued her—she found it be deep and otherworldly. She'd once asked Aleksei about the artist—who'd signed the initials "I.A." in one corner—but he'd been unwilling to reveal much about him or her, except to say quietly, "It's by an artist from the island where my family lives, who died some years ago."

He'd seemed reticent, meaning that he didn't want to talk about what could be a favorite retreat on his beloved home island of Naxea. Aleksei was an incredibly driven man and, apart from an endless stream of women passing through his life, he had to find his peace and relaxation somehow.

However, he was more willing to talk about the framed photos that also hung on his office walls, of bespoke, luxurious, architecturally cutting-edge Aegean villas, through which he'd built up his family's property business and made millions. He'd used his prowess to beat the economic crisis in southern Europe and sold or rented them to wealthy Americans and northern Europeans who sought spectacular second homes in the sun.

Shaking her head, she picked up the expensive tailored suit jacket he'd flung carelessly on the sofa where he'd met with his last clients. She laughed, thinking how much his informal manner belied his killer business instinct.

They used to meet daily, early in the morning, for him to brief her on what he needed done each day. She'd miss the way he leaned forward, sleeves rolled up, tanned forearms resting on the desk. He'd tug his tie loose, as though he couldn't stand it being tight, and unbutton the collar buttons. Even though he was all business, he kept in shape.

Her tummy flipped. In a couple of days, handsome, enigmatic, brilliant Aleksei would no longer be a part of her life.

This dynamic man she'd worked for over the last two years would have to be put behind her as she embarked on a new phase of her life.

Nostalgia had her turning away, but she stopped to straighten a pile of papers threatening to topple off a side chair. She tapped the last of the papers together and swung around, nearly bumping into Aleksei.

He reached out to hold her steady, but the warmth seeping through her thin blouse made her stiffen.

"Careful. It wouldn't do for you to have an accident and miss our dinner this evening."

His deep tones, flavored with his Greek heritage, washed over her. She raised her head and met his deep brown eyes, and a rush of heat bloomed in her cheeks. Wanting to cover her feelings for him, she laughed and retorted, "Oh, I'll be there, come what may, even if my leg is in a plaster cast and my arm is in a sling. I'm so looking forward to eating at Odyssea. They say the menu there is marvelous!"

His eyes crinkled into a heart-stopping smile. "Hopefully you'll make it through the next couple of hours in one piece, then," he said wryly. "The food at Odyssea is the best Greek cuisine in London."

He dropped his hands away from her and raked a hand through his thick ebony hair, a gesture she knew only too well meant he was moving into business dynamo mode again. "Did that call come through from Athens while I was in the meeting with Denise Ferguson?"

"No, not yet." She changed gears and responded with the efficiency and focus that he demanded. "But I did take another call from Phoenix Jones. I've left a note on your desk."

"*Na pari i eychi! Another* call? Can't the woman let it go?"

He paused, his jaw clenched, annoyance flaring in his dark eyes. But she had to tell him the truth. "I think Phoenix needs to be told that the relationship's over," she ventured carefully, giving a small grimace that conveyed her sympathy for both Aleksei and the uncomfortable task in front of him, and for Phoenix, whose pride was about to take a denting.

He surveyed her, his face a mask of control. Gusting out a heavy sigh, he held his hands up. "Yes, you're right. I'll speak to her now. After that, you'll deal with it in the usual way?"

"Yup. Let me know when you've talked to Miss Jones, and then I'll get on to it." *Good, finally taking my advice.* "What stones would you like?"

His features relaxed, and he chuckled. "Definitely rubies this time. She's one fiery lady. Set with diamonds, of course."

"Got it." She couldn't hide a rueful smile, agreeing with the fiery part. "Would you like some tea? I'm just about to make some for myself."

"*Efcharistó.* That would be most welcome." He paused and gave her a meaningful look. "You know, I'm going to miss you very much. I doubt if I'll find anyone as trustworthy and reliable as you ever again. Or as honest with me."

Her cheeks warmed again. "Oh, I'm sure you will." Suddenly shy, she batted away his compliment. "Susan Jenkins seems very professional and straightforward. She had no issues coping with the work when we did our handover day last week."

He pursed his lips. "She seems like a bit of a dragon to me."

"Aleksei!"

"Don't you think she looks a bit unapproachable and scary?"

She thought of Susan, a rather formal, starchy woman in her fifties, with her severe, short hairstyle, boxy suit, and clipped way of speaking. Even Phoenix Jones would have the devil's own job getting past her. "I think Susan will be perfect for what you need. She has years of experience working with CEOs of international corporations. I hand-picked her specially," she said diplomatically, adding hope-fully, "and she can't be that scary. She told me she breeds cats in her spare time."

"Cats? That is all right." He rubbed the back of his neck. "But I will miss you, Kate, very, very much." He paused. "Will you miss me?"

She hesitated. Longed to tell him that, yes, she would miss him with all her heart. But that kind of revelation wasn't part of their relationship and would do her no good at all. She fell back on humor to hide her sadness. "I think you'll miss me and my tea- and coffee-making skills more," she retorted sparkily.

For short seconds, his eyes lingered on her, then his mouth quirked into a smile. "We've made a good team, you and I. There will always be a place for you here, Kate. If you ever decide you want to return."

She nodded, tears gathering in her eyes. Hurrying out, she dabbed at her eyes. "I'll go make that tea."

Aleksei watched Kate's departing back. She would be irreplaceable. Bright, calm, and highly professional when the heat was on, there was no other woman in the world whom he could trust to be so open and direct with him. Many were the times he'd wondered what really went on under that capable, amusing exterior. A beautiful woman, with a creamy complexion, auburn hair, and sparkling aquamarine eyes, she held herself well—in a proud, determined, almost defiant way. But she was also something of a puzzle; her emotions were so very tucked away.

His body hardened, and he wondered once again what lay beneath her neat, quietly fashionable office outfits. What would it be like to undress her, to reveal her long, slender, exquisitely pale limbs, to kiss and caress her small, firm breasts? There was nothing false or fixed up about Kate.

He wanted her. But he'd never gone there, even though he could tell she wanted him as well—the way she broke eye contact too quickly, jumped like a nervous rabbit if he got too close, and tried too hard to be breezy and nonchalant if the conversation meandered to the personal. At times, the tension flickered between them like an elusive butterfly, and he could tell she found it hard to deal with.

No, she was classy, had been too valuable a colleague, too genuine a person, to lose because of a passing affair. Lovely as she was, it was better for a man like him to look but not touch. He preferred short-lived involvements with women who knew the score: sex, but no intimacy allowed.

Since she'd told him she was leaving, his physical desire for her had increased; what had once been an itch was spreading like a rash. But there was nothing to be done about it. It would be easy to seduce her now that her employment with him was coming to an end, but also dishonorable and messy.

He would not take advantage of the attraction he felt for her—or she for him. Though he had been wondering recently about the real reason she was leaving. His intuition signaled that she was inexperienced with men and, probably, she took things a little too much to heart. Perhaps he should probe a little further this evening, and reassure her that he was not the guy she should be wasting her affections on.

He sighed and went to sit at his desk. His cell lit up, showing that his stepsister was calling. He knew what about.

"Marina. How is it going? How are you feeling?"

"I'm very well, though getting bigger by the day."

Aleksei chuckled. "But that is good. The baby must be thriving. How is the proud father-to-be?"

"Still very proud and getting very excited. He can't stop buying things for the nursery. He's worse than me!"

Aleksei pictured his brother-in-law. He would be fine father material. He envied Adrastos. Here *he* was at thirty-five, and wishing more and more that he had children of his own. But he needed a permanent partner for that. "Are you calling to find out when I'll be home?"

"I am." Marina put on her stern voice. "Don't tell me that you won't be able to find time to return to Naxea this summer and greet your new nephew, Aleksei."

He laughed again. "You'll be amazed to hear that I have reserved the month of August as vacation time in my calendar, as usual. I'll be around for when you give birth. After all, this is a major event—the arrival of the heir to the Aleksanou dynasty. I wouldn't miss it for all the ouzo in Greece."

"Oh, that's terrific. I'm so glad." Marina's voice softened

with relief. "But what if the baby comes a little early?"

"It's no problem. Like I said, I just can't miss it."

He chatted with Marina some more and then ended the call. He was looking forward to going home to the island of his birth, being with family and having a break. Though all their childhoods had been difficult, he and his half-sisters were close. Sometimes he thought about relocating back there.

He brought his mind back to the present. Kate would be back with his tea soon. He had other calls to make—the first was that conversation with Phoenix Jones, which he'd rather not have, but, he was forced to concede, he owed her— before the close of business. Another woman who needed to be persuaded that he was not commitment material.

L ost in thought, Kate prepared a pot of tea in the small kitchenette adjoining their offices. She was going to miss her job at Aleksanou Associates, and Aleksei, a great deal, but it was right that she move on now. In her position as the gatekeeper of Aleksei's affairs, she'd become close to him in a certain way. She'd watched this man and learned the complexity of him: his passion for his business, his loyalty to his family, his humor under pressure, his ruthless determination to have exactly what he wanted—which included flexing his skill as a practiced seducer. He knew exactly how to stroke the female ego and make it purr. But at the first sign of real intimacy, it seemed, the shutters would come down; he bedded and discarded.

For a long time, Kate had relished their working

relationship, which had been characterized by a shared, focused approach to business during long working days and an easy professional friendship. But, in the last six months, teamwork with her darkly handsome boss had become a trial, and even sometimes a torture, as she'd realized that she had fallen for him.

Being so near to him and yet so far away was confusing and too painful to handle. So, when the opportunity had arisen for her to travel for a few months, she'd decided that she needed to seize it with both hands. She was like a pressure cooker waiting to explode, and there was nothing to be gained from mooning over him.

She retraced her steps to his office with the tea tray. He sat at his desk, talking on the phone in rapid Greek. As she placed his cup, he put a hand over the receiver and mouthed, "*Rubies.*" Obviously, he'd spoken to Phoenix. She returned to her desk and did her duty with the jeweler.

The table at Odyssea was booked for seven thirty p.m. It was true, she mused, as she pulled her makeup bag and comb from her purse to freshen up, that she'd often accompanied Aleksei to working lunches and dinners, acting as hostess to his numerous clients, but she'd never before sat down with him alone, socially, and she'd never really told him much about herself. She wondered what they would talk about tonight. Her trip around the Greek islands, she supposed.

Sometimes, on journeys back to the office in his limo after a meeting or a meal, or when a deal had been done, Aleksei had wound down, and she'd loved to hear his entertaining stories about the people he'd met or the places he'd been, or when he'd talked about his native Aegean island, Naxea. Indeed, it had been his rich descriptions of life there that inspired her to take her travel break in Greece. She would be seeing Naxea for herself soon, as she and her friend Lydia planned to stop there for a day or two toward the end of their three-month trip.

But what else?

She chewed her lip and reflected on the irony of having little to say to Aleksei now that she was finally going to be alone with him. *Lydia will know what to advise.* She ducked into the executive floor ladies' bathroom and speed-dialed her best friend on her cell.

Lydia was on her way home from work and ready to cheer Kate on.

"Just think, Katie, this is your moment! You've held a torch for him for so long and now you've got your chance to share an intimate dinner à deux with him!"

"But that's just it, Lyd. What will I say to him, what will we talk about? We can't discuss work stuff, and he keeps his private life so close to his chest."

"You've got loads to say. There's the trip…"

"And?"

"Well, tell him some other things about yourself."

"Oh, he's so going to be interested in me. A spinster living in a poky one-bedroom apartment in the suburbs, spending her weekends at the do-it-yourself store agonizing over paint."

"Come on, it's not that bad." Lydia protested. "You've got friends, you go out to bars, the cinema, the theater… sometimes."

"But that's hardly going to be interesting to someone who has a constant procession of supermodels gliding through his life."

"You could get all the gossip from him. Isn't he dating Phoenix Jones?"

"He wouldn't tell me anything in a million years. Anyway, Phoenix is toast. I sent her jewels about twenty minutes ago."

"Ah. What did she get?"

"Rubies."

"Wow. I wonder if you'll get a good-bye present."

"I haven't slept with him, Lydia."

"Well, perhaps you ought."

"Lydia!"

"Sorry, but I would. He's gorgeous, I bet he's brilliant in bed, and he gives big rocks as compensation. What's not to like?"

Kate paused. A vision of Aleksei, naked and making love to her, filled her mind. She shut it down quickly. "Seriously, Lydia, what am I going to do? He and I are poles apart when it comes down to it."

Lydia's tone gentled. "You know, Katie—and I've said this to you before—he's just a man, flesh and blood like you and me. You've allowed this unrequited love thing to grow into something humongous in your mind. But from what you've told me, he respects you and he's been a great boss. You like him. Just focus on that and the conversation will come."

Kate sighed. "That's good advice. I have let it get on top of me, haven't I? I guess it doesn't help that I haven't had a serious boyfriend for years."

"And we've got a plan to fix that, haven't we?" Lydia said brightly. "You're going to get back out there, start dating again. Maybe put a toe in the water with a nice holiday romance."

"I don't know…relationships and I just don't mix."

"Katie!" Now it was Lydia's turn to chide. "We've been over this again and again. What happened to you at uni was horrendous, but it was just one man, a long time ago, and you can't keep on hiding yourself away. You're a lovely, gorgeous, beautiful creature, and the men of the world are waiting for you."

Kate laughed, feeling better. Lydia never failed to cheer her up with her unbridled optimism. "Thank you. I've just got to work on repairing my confidence. I'm going to load my ereader with self-help books for while we're away and get my head together."

"That's the spirit. And you know what? My psychic instincts tell me that Greece will be the place where you find true love."

"Try some of this, it's very good." Aleksei offered a dip and the basket of pita bread to Kate.

How wrong she'd been to worry about not having much to say. From the minute they'd left the office, Aleksei had been perfect company, sweeping her along with his energy, wit, and charm. He'd made sure that the food, wine, and conversation flowed, and she understood more than ever why women stood in line to be with him; he wore charisma like other men wore cologne.

"Thank you," she responded gracefully, taking the piece of pita and dipping it in the eggplant mix. "Mmm. I just love the smoky flavor."

She licked a bit of dip off her lips. If she hadn't been looking at him, she'd have missed how his eyes dropped to her mouth. And lingered.

"I think we've tried all the meze now." He broke his stare, leaned away from the table, turned around and snapped his fingers. "Waiter, can you hurry up and bring the main courses? My personal assistant needs to sample your delicious lamb *kofta* next."

"I won't be *your* personal assistant for much longer," she pointed out and popped an olive into her mouth.

"Yes, more's the pity. Remind me, when do you go to Greece?"

"Our flight leaves Monday afternoon."

"Have you ever visited before?"

"No, this is my first time. If the food's as good as this, I think I'm going to love it."

He nodded. "Whenever you can, seek out the tavernas off the tourist track. Some of the more rural ones can serve the most delicious authentic dishes."

"Okay," Kate bubbled. "Though it sounds like I'll be coming home the size of an elephant after all that lovely grub."

He leaned back in his chair, and his eyes roamed over her again. "I'm sure there's no danger of that," he said softly. "You've got a great figure."

He paused, and the air shimmered between them. She felt both delighted and flustered by his compliment. The restaurant was crowded and noisy, and she suddenly felt hot. She searched for something to say, but nothing came.

He seemed to sense her unease and filled the gap. His dark brown eyes never left hers. "And you'll be backpacking, yes? All that walking and carrying will keep you slim."

"Oh…er…we'll be island hopping, so we're taking ruck-sacks… We can't take much, so I've been spending my last few evenings editing my traveling wardrobe. My friend and I have pledged to live the simple life while we're away." She paused to breathe again, aware she was babbling.

He smiled. "Greece is perfect for that. You'll be able to relax and unwind, which you thoroughly deserve after work-ing so hard for me."

"I am really looking forward to it. It's been a while since I had a vacation," she admitted.

"Are you? You've seemed a little subdued this past few days." He gave her a shrewd look.

Her breath caught in her throat. Surely he hadn't picked up on how she felt about him?

She scrabbled about for a reply that would deflect him. "There's been a lot to think about, what with letting out my apartment and the tricky business of packing my rucksack."

He looked at her quizzically, his head tilted on one side. "Well, knowing how many shoes you've got, it must be dif-ficult to restrict yourself to a few pairs." His mouth quirked upward.

He noticed my shoes? "How do you know that I've got loads of shoes?"

"You appear to wear a different pair to work every day."

"Not quite every day… Okay, I've had a really difficult time narrowing the contenders down for my trip," she admitted.

"But something's been bothering you, hasn't it? What is it? Having to leave your boyfriend behind?"

Kate swallowed. "Oh, I haven't got a boyfriend at the

moment," she said as casually as she could.

He leaned forward, apparently intrigued. "I can't believe that, Kate. A lovely girl like you. Surely there's someone special in your life?"

She looked down and fiddled with the edge of the snowy-white tablecloth. "No, there's nobody special right now." What could she say now to cover herself? Then she remembered her conversations with Lydia. She looked up again. "Maybe I'll meet someone while I'm traveling, have a vacation romance."

She thought she detected a glimpse of something dark flashing behind his eyes, but it passed quickly, though he still seemed quite serious. "Be careful, *pethi mou*. There are some nasty guys about. Make sure you choose wisely if you hook up with someone."

She was touched and amused by his slightly paternal advice. "I appreciate your concern, but don't worry. I'm quite fussy and, anyway, Lydia, my friend, will make sure I'm okay."

That last statement wasn't quite true. It was more likely to be Kate who would be keeping an eye on Lydia. She waited for Aleksei to reply, but he sat back in his chair and surveyed her silently, eyes narrowed.

She reached up and fiddled with her necklace, nervous about what he was thinking.

His eyes followed her movement and lingered.

She had to break the silence. "My dad's warned me about speaking to strange men, too," she joked.

Aleksei's dark brows knotted together. "You think I am like your father?"

"Well…"

"I'm offering good advice. You are too special to waste yourself on unworthy men."

She froze for a moment. Little did he know that she already had.

"What is wrong? Have I said something to offend you?"

She mentally shook herself. "No. Just feeling a little tired."

"All that shoe packing has worn you out, eh?"

"Something like that."

He reached across the table and took her hand, his touch sending a shock up her arm. She looked down at his hand, then up at him, and found herself held in his dark brown gaze. "I think you've been sad because you are going to miss me more than you care to admit, Kate."

She went rigid, and a flush of heat suffused her body. She forced her brain to think quickly. "I…yes, of course, I will miss working with you."

"I was thinking more than you will miss *me*." He stroked his thumb against her upturned palm. "In fact, I wonder if you are leaving because of me."

She'd been found out.

All the confusion and pent-up longing of the past few months welled up to the surface. *I'm a bloody idiot.*

His touch was seductive, making her hands clammy and her body melt. The understanding in his voice made her feel silly, somewhat ashamed, and vulnerable.

"You must think that I'm an idiot," she mumbled.

His thumb ran down her palm to her wrist, making her shiver. "I don't think you're an idiot at all. In fact, I think you are a very clever, sweet, beautiful woman, and if circumstances had been different, I would have wanted to get to know you better."

She looked at him, her eyes wide, startled by his admission. "Really?" she gasped. "I thought you never thought of me like that."

He smiled like a hungry panther. "Oh, I've thought of you, all right." He broke off for a minute, picked up his glass, and took a slug of wine. "I also noticed the attraction between us. You tried your best to hide it, but it was there."

Kate looked at the tablecloth, tried to collect her whirling thoughts and absorb what he was saying.

"It's hard to hide such feelings when two people work so closely together," he continued gently. "However, you are very different than other women I know—shy and modest by comparison."

"I thought...you would never be interested in me because of all the other...er...ladies you date. I'm not in the same league as them."

He shot her a look. "And all the better for it. For that reason, I never wanted to cross the line with you. You are too precious for that."

"I don't understand."

"I am as I am. I'm not cut out for long-term involvement, and you are not cut out for short-lived affairs. I would be no good for someone like you."

She sucked in a ragged breath and tried to steady herself. "But you did consider it?"

"I confess that I did. But I'm glad that I didn't."

"I see." She didn't know what else to say. She was punch-drunk with what he'd just told her. Aleksei Aleksanou was saying that he found her attractive!

He regarded her curiously. "What is it? Have I said

something to upset you?"

She looked up to see him scowling. "N-no!" She reached for her old friend, levity, in a crisis. "I just remembered I forgot to pack an important pair of sandals."

He laughed, reached for his glass, and raised it in a toast. "*Yamas!* Here's to your health, Kate. I wish you a wonderful, wonderful trip."

"Cheers!" she responded brightly and took a huge glug of her wine to still her beating heart. He found her attractive, but he hadn't made a move. He'd wanted to protect her. She didn't know whether to laugh or cry. The first part of that news made her want to punch the air, but the fact he'd also confirmed that she wasn't a woman who could tick his particular boxes stung her to the core, somehow…

Chapter Two

The following evening, Aleksei sat at his desk, reflective-ly tapping on its surface with a pen. Thoughts of last night's dinner with Kate had nagged at him all day. She'd been delightful company for most of it, and had opened up a little, although he was puzzled why she didn't appear to be dating at the moment. Afterward, he'd found it hard to sleep, thinking of her demure, flawless English rose looks and delicious, tall, slender body. He had to admit that his personal and professional codes that had made him stay at arm's length until now were starting to wear thin. He was so, so tempted...

But when he'd attempted to find out the real reason why she was leaving and also tell her the reason why her feel-ings were misplaced, he'd gotten the sense that he'd hurt her. She'd been vulnerable, then tried to joke it away, but he'd seen that she was upset. That had surprised him. He'd always thought of her as straightforward and realistic. Perhaps he'd revealed too much about his real emotions.

Then again, he always ended up hurting women's feelings. No matter how much they said they knew and accepted what the score was with him, ultimately they couldn't seem to deal with his truth.

He sighed, rubbed the back of his neck to ease his tense muscles. Kate had been unusually quiet and withdrawn today. It could have been because it was her last day and she was frantically busy finishing up, but he thought not.

His musings were interrupted by the buzzing of his phone. It was Kate, wanting to put a call through from Athens. He thanked her, then added, "Kate, it's six o'clock. Why don't you go and get ready for your leaving party now? I know you'll have left everything in apple-pie order."

"You don't need me to do anything after you've taken your call?"

"No," he said very definitely. "It can wait until Monday for Susan. Go and prepare to enjoy yourself."

Feeling a big pang because this was the last thing she'd ever do for him, Kate transferred the call, then heard his deep voice talking in the next room. He was already replacing her in his mind with Susan. He was moving on—and so should she.

But the shock of last night's conversation still lingered, laden with a bundle of muddled feelings. He'd admitted to finding her attractive, had said he'd thought about having an affair. He'd also been open with her about the fact that he didn't do commitment. After two years of working closely with him, she knew so very well that this last was true. She should have been pleased that her feelings were on some level reciprocated, maybe even liberated that she'd had a narrow escape. Knowing how she'd avoided relationships for the past few years, there was no way she would or could have gotten involved with him if he had asked. She would've found it too hard, because it would have inevitably ended, and she just couldn't have borne feeling the heart-stabbing pain of rejection again.

Perversely, though, finding out that her feelings for him hadn't been one-sided had only sharpened her desire for him—a desire that ached deep in her bones.

And that he saw her as too sappy to get involved with made her feel raw and sore.

She knew she was being contrary. It was that near-and-yet-so-far thing in one burningly concentrated hit. She could have been with him—he had wanted her. And yet she couldn't be with him, and ultimately he didn't want to be. Her head was tight with the tangle of it all.

But...deep down, a small voice of common sense implored her that there was absolutely no point in tearing at herself like this—she *had* to get a grip. She'd dreamed a dream, but now she knew the reality that lay behind it and she needed to shut it down, be sensible. She had a leaving party to go to, filled with nice people who would be wishing her well, and then a trip to make.

Mustering all her will, she reached for her tote bag, squared her shoulders, and rose from her desk, starting toward the ladies' room. After tonight it would be all over. Tomorrow, a new chapter of her life story would begin without Aleksei and, maybe, once she was away from him, the pain of wanting would begin to fade.

Twenty minutes, some freshly applied makeup, and a change of shoes later, Kate was standing outside the boardroom, opposite Aleksei's office. Already she could hear the sounds of music, lively chatter, and laughter: the party was in full swing. As she entered the room, a cheer went up among her coworkers and a few came forward to usher her into the throng.

She tried to relax as she chatted to her workmates, but she couldn't quite lose her feeling of edginess. She needed to chill. She accepted an offer from Brian, the lanky, bespectacled IT manager, to get her another drink. Watching Brian as he shambled across to the makeshift bar on the far side of the room, she also caught sight of Aleksei's tall frame, and her heart took a leap.

As much as she didn't want him to, he looked stunning in his bespoke suit, his bronzed features almost godlike in their perfect symmetry. He inclined his head slightly toward a female employee who was basking in his rare golden attention. He really did have the gift of making you feel as if you were the only person in his universe.

Suddenly, he looked up over the head of his chattering companion, and his eyes locked with hers. She thought she saw the spark of something in them and felt a strange kind of magnetic pull. Then he turned back to the woman to resume their conversation. Kate's throat ached—she wanted to be that woman. *Stop it.* She shook her head, trying to rid herself of her feelings of desolation.

Brian jabbed her arm, pressed a glass into her hand.

She downed the alcohol quickly and began to feel a little better—looser, more detached. When Brian offered to get her more drinks, she didn't refuse. Before long, she began to feel very warm and rather woozy. The room started spinning.

Perhaps she should have something to eat. Her meager lunch had been hours ago. She located the boardroom table, laden with a buffet of delicious party food. It seemed an awfully long way away.

Drawing herself up, she concentrated very hard on walking over, dimly aware that she was wobbling a little on her spike heels. She stumbled and found Brian at her side, ready to offer a steadying hand. She giggled and put her hand up to her hair in a gesture of embarrassment, but somehow got her ring caught up with one of her earrings and her efforts to shake it loose caused her carefully arranged updo to fall down around her shoulders in auburn waves.

"Oops," she giggled again.

Brian placed a hand on the small of her back and pushed her toward the buffet. "This way to the banquet, Lady Kate."

"Yes, I do fancy a nibble," Kate agreed recklessly, and noted in a hazy kind of way that Brian looked at her with raised eyebrows and a leer on his face. Her head was floating. Perhaps she was a little drunk. It was a nice feeling, and she couldn't help noticing how she was the center of attention—that spotty lad from accounts had joined them now, and a couple of other guys from sales and marketing. It was a shame it was so hot in here. She undid the top two buttons of her V-necked blouse.

"Lady Kate's treating us to a striptease," Brian said in his slightly nasal voice.

"Oh, you are awful," Kate told him cheerfully, pushing a hand at him and accidentally bumping his bony, concave chest.

His beady eyes lit up behind his specs.

A cross the room, Aleksei watch the hubbub gathering around his ex-personal assistant. There was a growing group of male employees, all of them mesmerized by the tall, slender woman in their midst.

Something must be wrong. She normally never talked and laughed that loudly, or threw her arms about. Her hair tumbled around her shoulders, and her normally pale cheeks were flushed. Even from across the room he could see the creamy swell of her breasts covered by a strip of lace.

Christos! He didn't hesitate and moved swiftly across the room, slicing through the crowd to place a guarding hand under her elbow. "It's getting a little warm in here, and Kate needs some air."

He turned to the men standing by gawping and gestured at the food-laden table. "Help yourselves," he invited. "We'll be back in a moment." With that, he propelled an unsteady Kate from the room, retrieving her glass from her. "I'll take care of that."

In the cool of the hallway, he leaned her up against the wall, keeping a supportive hand around her waist.

Straightening, he looked at her heated face and glazed expression. "You look a little flushed. I'll get you some water."

She giggled again, pulling at the buttons of her blouse with one hand and theatrically fanning herself with the other. "You don't know how hot I am," she slurred.

His eyebrow shot up. "Oh, I think I do." His eyes traveled

down to the still-exposed expanse of her chest. "Come here." He drew the edges of her blouse together and tried to cover her breasts.

He couldn't help that his hand brushed her skin, and he saw how she jolted. He looked up, and their eyes met. He carefully withdrew his hands from her, and her own flew back to the gaping material. He took a much needed step back.

A pretty blush suffused her cheeks.

"**O**h, no! I..." She shuddered to a halt. "I've made a complete fool of myself. Oh, God, I'm so sorry..."

"No, you haven't. You've just had a bit too much to drink, that's all. Why don't you go and tidy yourself up, and I'll get you that water."

"Okay...thank you." Mortified, she averted her gaze to the carpet. She clutched her open top and shuffled toward the loo. She put a steadying hand on the wall.

The ladies' was empty, thank goodness. She walked unsteadily to the sink and concentrated on placing the plug in the basin. Letting the cold water run, she peered at herself in the wall mirror, staggering a little. The sight that greeted her wasn't pretty. Her eyeliner and mascara had smudged, there was a visible shiny slick of perspiration in the valley between her breasts, one earring was missing, and her hair had fallen in rat tails around her shoulders.

Flashes of her behavior popped into her brain like a succession of camera takes. She gripped the edge of the basin. Not normally a great drinker, she'd become intoxicated very quickly. She'd been hungry and miserable, and the alcohol had gone straight to her head. Like a floozy, she'd shown her bra to the world! She wondered what Aleksei would think and wanted to crawl into a hole.

She fumbled to turn off the tap and splashed her face liberally with cold water, dampening her blouse even more. She dabbed clumsily at her panda eyes with a tissue and attempted to comb her hair back from her face with her fingers. Not great, but at least better.

As she carefully negotiated her way outside into the hallway again, she thanked her lucky stars when she saw it was deserted. Perhaps she could slip away without anyone noticing. Aleksei had placed a glass of water on a console table. She went over to it, sliding a hand along the wall to support herself. Her head swam, beginning to ache.

She raised the glass to her lips, but a pair of hands curved around her waist from behind. She lost her balance and spilled water down her front.

"Hey, Lady Kate, still fancy a bit of a nibble?" Brian asked in his nasal twang.

His hot breath made her cringe, and his hands tightened in a painful grip around her middle. His fat wet lips landed on the side of her neck.

"Did you know you look a lot like the other Kate— Duchess of Cambridge? Except that she hasn't got such lovely red hair," he breathed in her ear again.

"If you don't let go of me, I'll…I'll give you a right royal kick!" she shrieked, struggling to free herself from his groping hands and reptilian mouth, but he clung on fast and she only succeeded in falling forward and head butting herself against the wall.

His damp paw clamped onto her breast, and he reeked of alcohol as he tried to smear kisses down the side of her face.

Then, in a split second, Brian was gone. A movement beside her made her turn, and she saw the IT manager being slammed face-first against the wall by a strong tanned hand.

Aleksei held Brian by his jacket collar. "If I could kill you I would, you little creep." He loosened his grip on Brian's collar so that the craven man slid away down the wall, his spectacles dropping off his nose. "But we live in the civilized world of business, where uncivilized men like you, who force themselves on women, will not be tolerated. So, instead of having the pleasure of taking you apart piece by piece, I will be handing you over to HR, who will take the appropriate course of action to terminate your employment." He whipped out his phone with his free hand, deftly scrolled up a number and barked something in guttural Greek.

When his phone call was done, and while continuing to dangle Brian limply by his jacket collar, he looked at her. "Are you okay? Did he hurt you?"

"I'm…I'm fine," she managed as she shrank up against her small patch of wall.

Aleksei surprised her by reaching out to sweep a fallen lock back from her forehead. "You don't look fine. You have a small bump forming there. You must have hit the wall hard."

The concern in his voice and the gentle brush of his fingers against her face were too much. A huge ball of emotion rose in her throat, and tears welled in her eyes. She swallowed hard. "I'm okay…really."

Two burly members of the security team came pounding around the corner, and within a short space of time, escorted

Brian away.

She couldn't hold back the tears, and she emitted a small sob. Her head fell forward, and she buried her face in her hands.

Aleksei's arms wrapped around her, and he stroked her hair. "Hush," he soothed, although his voice was gruff. "It's okay. It's all right. I've got you."

A dam burst inside her, and tears flowed free. The rhythmic strokes on her back calmed her, and she allowed herself to nestle into his broad chest and breathe in the lemon-whiskey male scent of him.

"I'm so sorry…I didn't mean…I didn't know what I was doing," she whispered.

"I know," he said. "I know." His hand stilled, then pulled back from her. He shrugged off his suit jacket and held it out to her. "Here, put this on. You're shivering."

"I am a bit damp. Thanks."

"I think we need to get you home. I'll get Tino to collect your coat and bags. My car is waiting for us at the front of the building."

She thought about saying good-bye to her colleagues who, from the sounds of chat and merriment that floated along the corridor, were still partying away in the boardroom. But no way did she want to go back inside and face all those people.

Yawning, and still a bit tipsy, she just wanted to go to bed. Her head throbbed from bumping it on the wall. She let herself be guided toward the elevator.

Once inside, he jabbed the button for the ground floor, and they traveled down in silence. She could feel his glance glide over her, but she continued to look straight ahead. She closed her eyes and her head spun, until the stopping of the lift and the touch of his hand at her elbow jolted her back to reality, and the doors opened onto the dimly lit foyer.

"Come," he said, holding back the elevator doors. When her feet refused to walk in a straight line, Aleksei helped her take off her stilettos. Carrying her shoes and putting an arm around her, he guided her out across the smart marbled hall to the glass-fronted entrance and down the steps to where his private limousine driver waited at the curb.

The car sped through the brightly lit London streets filled with Friday night revelers. When Kate caught sight of her disheveled state in the window reflection, a cloud of shame descended over her.

He slid an arm along the back of the seat and squeezed her shoulder. "Don't distress yourself about what happened tonight. You can rest assured that Brian will be dealt with."

His touch comforted her, warmed her inside. "You're not going to sack him, are you?"

His lips thinned. "You're too nice for your own good. The guy tried to assault you. He's lucky that you're not pressing charges."

"No, I don't want to do that," she said quickly.

"So firing him is the right thing to do."

"I guess." She heaved a sighed. "You must think I'm a lush. Honestly, I don't usually drink much, and I didn't mean to get so hammered and make such a display of myself."

The words came tumbling out in a rush and he put a hand over hers to silence her. "Don't worry about it. You were tired and emotional, and probably hungry. You didn't really get time to eat lunch today, you were so busy finishing up. And like you say, you're not used to drinking alcohol."

His hand, brown and large, remained over hers. She found herself looking into his handsome face, taking in its lean hard planes and his dark, steady gaze.

"Thanks for being so understanding, and thanks for taking me home like this," she said in a small, wobbly voice. "I really appreciate it. I don't think I could have negotiated a taxi."

"You're welcome." He inclined his head. "That's what friends are for." He waggled her hand affectionately and trailed his palm up her fingers. He smiled at her, then turned to look silently out of the window. Touched by the gesture, she watched his profile for a while, then lay back and closed her eyes, snuggling into the buttery softness of the leather seat.

She must have dropped into a doze because, before she knew it, Aleksei was gently shaking her awake. "You're home."

"Oh." She roused herself and slid out of the limo into the fresh night air, which made her head spin once more. The chauffeur walked around the limo and gathered up her belongings for her. Barefoot, she walked carefully up the garden path and then fumbled for the key in her purse.

She glanced behind her. Aleksei had followed her and stood waiting.

"Thanks for bringing me home…"

He held up a hand to stop her. "I think I'd better come in, don't you? You're still a little inebriated, there's a swelling the size of a turkey egg on your forehead, and I don't want you getting into difficulties in the middle of the night. If you vomit, I'll need to take you to hospital."

She peered at him in the dimly lit entrance. "You're… staying over?"

"That's my plan."

"But—but I've only got one bedroom."

His mouth turned up at one corner. "You've got a couch as well, I presume?"

"*Yes...*"

"Then that's fine. All I need is the couch, the bathroom, and a cup of coffee." He gestured to her to open the front door.

Befuddled and bemused, she did as she was bidden but found it hard to aim the key into the lock. After a minute or so, he took it from her and let them both into her first-floor apartment.

He guided her into the hallway. "This is nice." He strode through to the large kitchen-diner that was combined with the living-room into one large open-plan space and turned on the light. "You've got a backyard," he observed, looking at the French windows at the far end of the room.

"A patio," she mumbled, wincing at the bright light.

"Very nice," he repeated. "Now what about that coffee?"

She waved an unsteady hand in the direction of the kitchen area and took a step backward to steady herself.

"It's okay, I'll do it," he volunteered. "You just go and sit down."

She shuffled over to the couch and plonked herself down. "Could you get me a glass of water? I've got a real headache."

He came over to her and squatted down on his haunches, then examined her forehead with strong brown fingers, gingerly prodding the swelling there. "You have a bruise forming. How about some anti-inflammatory painkillers? They'll also help with the aftereffects of tonight's revelry."

She nodded slowly. "They're in the kitchen cupboard… over the sink."

"Okay." He made his way over to the kitchen, opened and shut a few cupboard doors, located a tumbler and the painkillers. He brought them back, the glass filled with water, and proffered them to her. "Why don't you stretch out for a while?"

She put her feet up on the couch and lay back gratefully into the pillowy cushions. She could hear him preparing fresh coffee behind her, and eventually the aroma filled the small space. He seemed perfectly at home. "Try not to throw up," he instructed her cheerfully, "and let me know if the pain in your head gets any worse."

She grunted and then fell asleep.

When Kate awoke, the sun was up and the birds were singing their morning chorus. She sat up and her head swam. She groaned and rubbed at the headache throbbing in her skull. She lay back down again. Her mouth tasted horrible. Then she noticed that she was in her bed, still fully clothed, though nicely tucked in under her quilt. *How did I get here?*

The sound of water splashing reached her. *Aleksei?* She hauled herself up, resisting the urge to collapse once more, swung her legs over the side of the bed, and staggered to her feet, making her way to the bathroom.

The door stood open, and she stopped short.

Aleksei.

Naked.

In *her* shower stall.

The force of his sheer maleness hit her like a punch. Her head reeled, and she stopped breathing for a few seconds. He had his back to her, the muscles of his broad shoulders rippling. Streams of water and shower gel trickled down a broad expanse of brown skin to his lean, firm buttocks and long sturdy legs.

He turned around.

She sucked some much-needed air into her lungs and continued to stand mesmerized, unable to tear her eyes away from the liberal sprinkling of coarse dark hair that covered his chest, then arrowed its way down his superbly defined six-pack to…

"Good morning," he said cheerfully, apparently not in the least fazed, his mouth curving into a heart-stopping smile. He flicked off the faucet and reached out to grab a large towel, casually slung it round his waist. "How are you feeling?"

"Um, still a little shaky…" she managed. "Um, I'll go make us some tea." She grabbed her toothbrush and the tube of toothpaste, turned and fled to the kitchen. She went to the sink and hurriedly brushed her teeth there, then stared into space for some minutes, remembering the sight that she'd seen in the bathroom, clutching at the basin for support.

The tea was brewing when he appeared, fully dressed, unshaven, but clean and relaxed. Kate was acutely aware of her crumpled clothes and bushy hair.

"This is so very English, having tea at breakfast," he remarked.

"Would you prefer some coffee?" She made a distracted, half-hearted attempt at running her fingers through her mussed hair.

"No, tea's fine. A nice change for me," he replied. Then he gave her a speculative look. "Why don't we go sit down on the couch? You do look rough."

"Thanks for letting me know," she replied grumpily and concentrated on getting the tea things together on a tray, then carried them over to where he'd seated himself. Anticipating he was going to say something about last night, she decided to get in there first.

"I would like to apologize for my behavior last night," she said solemnly, settling onto the couch. "And to thank you for coming to my rescue."

He smiled. "Don't look so downhearted. I know that it was out of character for you, and everybody slips up once in a while."

"But the thing with Brian…"

"Not your fault. No one should take advantage of another person while they are not fully in control. It was his behavior that was unforgivable, and he will be dealt with in the correct way. Forget him!"

She smiled and busied herself pouring the tea, then offered milk and sugar. For a while, they sipped in silence, Kate trying desperately hard to get the image of him naked in the shower out of her head and not succeeding. As bad as she felt, her desire for the man was bigger than ever. And in a few minutes, he'd be gone forever. Suddenly, she felt incredibly emotional and covered with an overwhelming sense of loss. *Oh, God…*

Sure enough, his tea finished, he stood up and collected his jacket from the back of the couch. He appeared withdrawn and uneasy now. "I guess I'd better be on my way. Will you be okay?"

She eased herself up and nodded. "If I feel unwell, I'll phone Lydia. She doesn't live far away."

There was another silence. She couldn't stop the emotion from welling up inside her; her heart began to pound and a lump formed in her throat.

He seemed to sense her distress and without warning took her hands and pulled her toward him in an embrace.

Her arms wrapped around him, and she buried her face in his chest, inhaling his soapy smell, feeling the warmth and safety of him. At the same time, her need for him began to spiral.

He squeezed her tight. They stayed like that for what seemed like minutes, then he pulled away from her and stroked her hair.

"*Pethi mou*, you are one special lady. Take care of yourself. If you ever need anything, you know where I am."

Then he surprised her by placing a kiss on her cheek.

She savored the feel of his lips as they feathered against her skin, the gentle caressing of his hands in her hair, and she couldn't help nuzzling against him.

He inhaled sharply. He cupped her head, his fingers strong, yet gentle. He kissed her hungrily.

She responded with equal fervor, like a parched woman slaking her thirst at a desert oasis. His tongue probed her mouth, and she opened up to him, wanting more, more…

Her hands roamed the muscles of his broad back, her mind flashing images of his nakedness and pushing her on.

Finally, he broke contact with her and stepped away. With one last brush of her cheek, he turned wordlessly away and left her apartment, leaving her standing there.

Chapter Three

Saturday was a bit of a lost day for Kate. She felt hungover for most of it, and dislocated, as the reality of quitting Aleksanou Associates set in. She'd been so driven to end the agony of her unrequited feelings for Aleksei, she hadn't stopped to think through how she would feel about actually leaving him or the job she'd loved. And even worse, she still felt very uncomfortable about how drunk she'd gotten last night.

But more than any of that, the memory of Aleksei's kiss was seared on her brain—the way his mouth had told her of his intense physical power and need for her. She'd never experienced anything like it.

In the end, to stop it going round and round in her head, she decided to have an afternoon nap. But when she awoke feeling as off beam as she had an hour before, she invited Lydia over and ordered Indian takeout.

"So, how far have you gotten with your packing?" Lydia

asked through a mouthful of curry and rice.

"I've just about finished," Kate replied, sighing, pushing her korma around her plate with her fork. "I've just got to pop out tomorrow and get some travel-sized toiletries and some sun protection, come home and clean up here, and then I'm done. I should have gone shopping today, but I just didn't feel up to it."

"You can always buy stuff when you get there," Lydia suggested, helping herself to a bit hunk of Peshawari naan bread.

"Yeah, I guess. But I'll feel happier setting off with a basic set." Kate put her fork down. "You can't always get high-SPF cream in the Mediterranean."

"And all your closets and drawers are cleared for my brother and girlfriend to come and apartment-sit while we're away?"

"Yup, it's all packed away and put into storage."

"What's wrong?" Lydia peered at her friend, looking concerned. "You're on the eve of one of the greatest adventures of your life and you sound so...*un*excited."

"I'm still tired and dehydrated a little after my um... binge...last night."

Lydia giggled. "I know you don't think so, but it was so funny the way you told it. Especially the part when Aleksei dangled Brian by his collar and his specs started sliding down his nose."

"No, I don't think it's funny at all. It was humiliating." She was tired, weary of the whole evening that wouldn't stop replaying in her mind.

"But you got to see Aleksei in the shower, *naked*. Wasn't that worth all the humiliation in the world?"

Once again, Kate was assailed by a vision of his big, fit, tanned body. She lowered her eyelids to try and block it out and was surprised to find when she opened them again that her eyes were brimming with tears.

"Oh, Katie!" Lydia plonked her meal down on the coffee table and rushed to wrap her arms around her weeping friend. "I was only joking."

"I know. But it just reminds me that I'll never see him again... He kissed me, Lyd. I...I want him...I want him more than ever!"

Lydia gave her a comforting squeeze. "I know, I know. But he's a heartless womanizer, and you don't do relationships, remember?"

She paused and looked up at her friend through blurry eyes. "I know." She sniffed, reached for a tissue and blew her nose. "But, somehow...where he's concerned, I've gotten past my inhibitions. I want him and I can't stand the thought of not seeing him again." She took a deep breath. "If he were to come through that door right now and demand to make love to me, I'd say yes, if it would mean that I had a little piece of him for just a while longer."

Lydia sat back and whistled, making the hair around her forehead blow upward. "Blimey, you have got it bad, girlfriend! Is this really the born-again virgin Kate Burrows talking?" She stopped and put her head on one side. "This is probably very bad advice, as it comes from me...but some-times it's best not to overthink everything and just follow your heart."

Kate tried to smile, then started to choke as the tears flowed again. "But there's no chance of him walking through the door, is there? It's all fantasy. He's gone...for good."

Now the tears turned into sobs, and she was grateful Lydia sat there patting her shoulder, letting her cry it all out.

The next morning, Kate awoke feeling calmer. She'd had a good howl last night, and it had helped to voice her feelings. She'd accepted that her feelings were just...*feelings*. After all her time spent in her emotional deep freeze, she needed to thaw slowly before getting involved with any man again. And, anyway, Aleksei was no longer part of the life. She had to get real and move on.

Hopefully, once she was in Greece, she'd be able to get him out of her system. Today she was just going to take it slowly: focus on her trip, pamper herself in readiness, have a nice leisurely breakfast, and then head out to the shops. Then she had to do some cleaning in anticipation of her tenants taking possession of her apartment while she was away.

She was just rubbing in her favorite body lotion when the doorbell rang. *Lydia?* Perhaps she'd left something behind last night. She hurriedly wrapped her robe around herself as she made for the front door.

The doorbell rang again, this time more insistently. When she pulled the door open, she froze.

Aleksei, dangling the spike-heeled shoes she'd been wearing on Friday night.

"Hello," he drawled, delivering one of his heart-stopping smiles. "My chauffeur found these on the backseat of the limo." Then he seemed to register her state of undress. "I appear to have called at an inconvenient time."

"Oh...no, it's fine. Please do come in." She backed up,

bumping into the wall, to let him pass by into the hallway.

"Only if you're sure?"

"Yes, it's fine. I was just about to make coffee." Kate ushered him in, quickly grabbing the edges of her robe when they parted after the gesture.

"How are you feeling?" he asked when they reached the living room.

"Oh, way better, thank you," she responded too brightly. "Thank you for returning my shoes. I'd totally forgotten about them."

"Yes, so had I." A smile playing around his mouth. "But Charlie found them when he was cleaning out the limo."

He leaned against the kitchen counter, arms stretched behind him, biceps bulging under his shirtsleeves. She kept glancing at his tall frame, clad in a powder-blue cotton shirt, sleeves rolled up to his elbows. The top three buttons were undone, exposing his tanned chest and a slash of dark chest hair. His hair looked windblown, not tame as it usually was. And he hadn't shaved.

Why, oh, why does he have to look so hot with a five o'clock shadow? She swallowed. Hard. Warmth snaked through her pelvis, something she hadn't felt in a very long time.

"Okay, coffee's ready." She brushed past him to fix the tray, and her robe flapped open to expose her thigh. She grabbed at it to retain her modesty, pulling the edges together again and adjusting the belt. Picking up the kettle, she prepared their drinks.

Although her back was to him, she could feel him staring at her. Her damp, heavy hair flopped in an unruly tumble around her shoulders. She straightened, wishing that her robe would stay wrapped around her. She stood as well as she could in a dignified pose.

Silence ensued, Aleksei staring at her.

It reminded her of the calm before a thunderstorm, when the birds stopped singing and the heavy became warm, thick and heavy.

"I've got to go and get dressed," she blurted out. She made to go past him, but his outstretched hand stopped her in her tracks.

"Kate." He slid his hands up her arms to her shoulders, stopping her mad dash.

She looked up at him, mesmerized by his dark eyes.

He raised one hand from her shoulder and brushed a lock of hair from her face. "So this is how you really are—without your smart business suits, tied-back hair, and make-up. Fresh, vulnerable, and so very tempting."

A tremor shook her, but not out of fear. She forced her eyes downward, thrown so far out of her comfort zone and wanting to run to safety. The way he was touching her, looking at her, she knew something was going to happen, but for the life of her, she was powerless to call a halt.

He lifted her chin, forcing her to meet his gaze again. "I want you," he breathed, then he lowered his mouth to hers and kissed her gently.

His lips sipped at hers. Lifting his head back an inch, his eyes roamed over her face. "I've been wondering how you would look naked. What it would be like to uncover your skin, make love to you."

"Aleksei…I…"

He brushed her lips with his again, silencing her. "You've seen me naked. I think you liked what you saw." He pulled her to him again and captured her mouth, coaxing it to open. His tongue swept in, exploring her mouth, slowly at first, then with a raw need that knocked the air from her lungs.

She yielded to the strength of him, pressing her body urgently against his. Giving up the battle to keep her robe covering her body, she let it go and raised her hands to his head. His hair was softer than she'd thought it would be, and she delighted in running her fingers through it.

The robe fell away, and his hands swept down the length of her spine to cup her buttocks.

"*Christos*, Kate, you have no idea how much I've needed to do this."

Somehow he knew every sensitive place on her bare body, expertly caressing her. Her hardened nipples chafed against his shirt, sending sparks of desire through her belly.

He tilted her head, deepening the kiss, and cupped her breast. He kneaded it with skillful, rhythmic moves.

Needing to find her balance, she stepped back and made contact with the kitchen unit, taking him with her, their mouths still firmly locked together.

He pressed her against the granite top, used his thigh to nudge her legs apart.

She moved against him in response, as he bent and sought her nipple with his mouth. Flames licked her skin, and she thought she could climax just from his mouth doing such delicious things.

For how long he held her there, she couldn't say. All she could feel was his mouth and hands on her breasts, and the molten liquid that was pooling at the apex of her thighs.

He lifted his head, his hooded eyes met hers. He gently swept her hair back from her face. "Oh, God, Kate." He bent and swept her up into his arms, carried her to the bedroom.

She threw her arms around his neck and buried her face in his chest. This was where she wanted to be. She couldn't hold back the months of stored-up hunger, of longing for him anymore.

He took her to her bed and put her down gently. She lay there naked, all self-consciousness disappeared, as he stared down at her. He peeled off his shirt and then his pants and boxers, keeping his eyes locked with hers.

She noted the fabulous muscular lines of his taut bronzed body and his magnificent erection. Her body throbbed, ached, begged for him to touch her.

The way he stared at her was too much, and she closed her eyes, afraid he'd see just how much she wanted him.

"Look at me," he commanded, and her eyes flew open again. "Open your legs, *pethi mou*. Don't hide from me anymore. Let me see you."

Hesitantly, she parted her legs slightly, and his eyes followed the movement. Coming to kneel down beside her on the bed, his hand slipped between her thighs, first stroking the soft skin there, moving to slide in a finger and gently caress her taut nub.

She gasped and closed her eyes once more, arching her back, rising up to meet his hand as waves of pleasure washed over her.

"Does that make you feel good?" he whispered. His strokes intensified, circling faster. He reached up to take both her wrists in his hand, holding her fast, continuing his delicious torture. He slid a finger inside her, then two, and she bucked, so close to coming apart in his hands. She threw her eyes open and looked up at him, pleading with her eyes.

"Oh, Aleksei, please…please," she whispered.

His fingers stilled, then withdrew. He said nothing, but a half smile quirked around his mouth as he gazed at her. Moving his body over hers, he captured her mouth in a searing kiss. Cupping her bottom toward him, he entered her with one swift movement.

She tensed for a moment, expecting tightness and discomfort, but instead felt no pain. Wrapping her legs around his waist, she welcomed him deeper, his hot, hard flesh sending her to new heights. Every thrust seemed to reach deeper and deeper. On and on, further and further, higher and higher…

She exploded into what seemed to be an endless vortex of ecstasy.

He tensed above her and groaned, his own climax taking over his movements.

They lay quiet, breathing hard, still joined together. He caressed her, making lazy circles on her shoulder, covering her face and neck with little kisses. He pulled away and rolled over beside her, pulling her into his arms.

She laid her head on his chest and listened to his thumping heart slow and resume normal rhythm. After a while, his breathing evened out, and she knew he'd fallen into a sated sleep.

But she stayed wide-awake, her body still tingling from his expert lovemaking. Her mind raced. It was hard to believe that she was here, now, in bed with him—the very thing that she had dreamed of but thought would never happen…had happened!

Lightly, so as not to waken him, she caressed the dark silky hair on his chest and across his brown skin, almost to prove to herself that he *was* here and it had been *real*.

She had been intimate with Aleksei—and it was mind-blowing.

But then another, darker thought came flooding in. What had happened to that fragile protective shell she'd kept intact around her, shielding herself from all emotional and physical involvement, for years since…since…?

She tried to swallow the hard lump in her throat. She turned to look at him, fast asleep and illuminated by the fingers of sunny morning light that crept through the wooden blinds.

So beautiful he took her breath away.

Then she remembered real life, and her heart sank. Her previous two years spent as his right-hand woman, and also their recent conversation, had underlined the drill, for goodness' sake. The man was a serial seducer; he didn't do commitment. No strings, no demands, no clinging—and he applied those rules to women who were far more glorious trophies than she.

It struck her then that they hadn't used protection… Oh, sweet Lord!

She willed herself to slide out of bed. She sneaked another look at his sleeping form, his powerful bronzed body unveiled by the pushed-back quilt, his arm flung out across the pillows as he breathed evenly and rhythmically, and saved the memory in her mind. Then she grabbed her robe and headed for the bathroom.

About half an hour later, she went to wake him with a mug of coffee. She placed it on the bedside table and leaned over, gently shaking his shoulder. "Aleksei…"

His eyelids fluttered open. "Hey," he said sleepily, then

his hand rose up, pulled her down to sit on the bed and touched her cheek. "You okay, sweetheart?"

She smiled and tilted her head to one side. He actually looked relaxed, more relaxed than she'd ever seen him. "Yes, I'm great," she said, faux happy.

"I'm great, too," he replied, stroking her cheek. Then his expression changed, and he sat up and looked at his watch. "*Christos!* I have to go, *pethi mou*. I have a meeting up in town."

"On a Sunday?" she asked, a little taken aback by his swift change of pace and mood.

"Yes, Stavros Constantinou is here today on his way back to Athens from New York, remember? I have to talk to him about the Ithaca project."

"Oh. Yes. I remember now. I booked lunch for you and him at your favorite Chinese restaurant in the West End." Disappointment welled up in her chest.

He chuckled. "Stavros is Greek, but he loves Chinese food." He stirred. "I'd better get going if I'm to get up there by one."

"Of course." She moved out of the way to let him out of bed, trying hard to beat down the feelings that were urging her to beg him to stay. What had she expected? This was Aleksei. He didn't do commitment.

His phone beeped. He rummaged in his chinos pocket, checked the screen and muttered to himself. Then he swiped the screen again and threw the handset down on the bed next to her.

She watched him as he turned his back to her and swiftly dressed. She couldn't help it as her eyes wandered to the phone, which lay screen up. There was a list of text messages.

At the top of it was the name Phoenix Jones, today's date, and the time of arrival—about a minute ago, and the first part of the text: *Hi, baby, looking forward to seeing you tonight.*

She froze.

Clearly Phoenix hadn't taken her marching orders…

Dressed, he turned around and walked toward the bed. He leaned down and gave her a lingering kiss on the mouth. "Got to go. Take care, *pethi mou*. If you ever need me…"

She gave a tight little nod and forced a smile. And then he was gone.

The next morning, the doorbell shrilled at six thirty. Lydia wasn't due to arrive for another half an hour, when they would make their way to the airport. Oh, well, at least everything was ready even if Lydia was early. Despite being exhausted after the events of the weekend, she'd made a final effort yesterday after Aleksei left to finish packing, go shopping, and clean up. Her large rucksack sat packed by the front door, and the apartment was ready and waiting for her temporary tenants to take up residence while she traveled.

She hurried to answer the door and found a courier standing there holding a small package. "Miss Burrows?" He handed the delivery to her and, having gained her signature of acceptance, was off along the front path. Kate stood looking at the neatly wrapped package for a few seconds—what on earth could this be?

She went back inside and shut the door. Unwrapping

it, she discovered a small box wrapped with a silk ribbon, inscribed with the name of a very fashionable jeweler on its lid. A small card addressed to her lay just beneath the ribbon. She knew that handwriting. She opened it and read the message: "*We made a good team. Bon voyage. Aleksei.*"

Inside the little box was a bracelet of tiny gold links in the shapes of Greek keys, inset with small turquoise and coral stones.

It was exquisite and unique. But a knife turned, sharp, in her heart. Jewelry was Aleksei's signature parting gift to all his lovers. After all, she'd ordered it often enough on his behalf when the time had come for him to say good-bye and move on from his latest affair.

Yesterday morning, all her instincts had told her not to cling—and she'd been right. *Aleksei doesn't do commitment.*

Chapter Four

"For someone who's spent ten weeks vacationing in the sun, you look pretty peaky and wan." Lydia eyed Kate with concern.

They were seated outside at a harbor-front café, waiting for breakfast to arrive.

Kate couldn't deny that she felt rotten. "I think that stomach bug must have come back again."

"Don't you think you ought to see a doctor now that we're here on Naxea for a few days? You've been poorly on and off for the last four weeks—you're looking exhausted and pale and you're dead to the world by ten o'clock most nights."

Guilt reared its head again. Their plan of hitting the bars and clubs of every island they'd visited had fizzled away over the last month or so, because she'd been feeling so sick and exhausted. "Oh, Lyd, I'm sorry. I've been a real drag, haven't I?"

Lydia waved a dismissive hand. "No, you haven't! I've had some grand adventures exploring the nightlife of the Kephelades islands on my own. But it would have been good to spend more nights dancing round our purses with you—we always have a laugh. I'm just worried about you, that's all."

Kate managed a smile, though it coincided with the waiter delivering their breakfast to them. The sight and the smell of thick Greek yogurt, honey, crusty bread, fruit, and coffee should have been appetizing, but her stomach just heaved, and she made a hasty exit to the loo.

After a while, she felt a little better and went back to join Lydia at the table outside, but stopped at the café doorway and watched her friend scoffing a hearty breakfast, looking tanned and glowing. It was time she faced up to the possibility that had been haunting her over the last several weeks: two missed periods, vomiting, and tiredness. In all likelihood, she was pregnant.

Her breath caught in her throat for a moment as unbidden images of Aleksei rose up in front of her. All holiday, thoughts of him—masculine, strong, so darkly mesmerizing as he'd made love to her—had haunted her days and brought pleasure to her dreams. She gripped the chair next to her to steady herself. What if she was expecting his baby?

She shook her head slightly, as if to rid herself of the pictures in her head, and concentrated on walking back out to the table, pretending she was calm. "Lyd. You're right. I'm going to go to the pharmacy over there, maybe get something for my stomach." She pointed to the small row of shops along the harbor's edge. "I'll also ask them where the nearest doctor's surgery is, just in case."

She set off across the cobblestones. The pharmacist was a charming woman who spoke good English. She presented Kate with a pregnancy test as requested and gave her directions to a clinic, though Kate doubted she would visit it; she'd be back in London in a fortnight and would visit her own GP then. But at least she could take the test in order to stop wondering and start thinking about what to do next.

Clutching the box that would confirm her fate, she emerged from the store into the bright sunlight and was disoriented. A loud motor revved, and she glanced up as a boy on a scooter sped toward her. She tried to take evasive action and dodge the boy, but he came too fast, snatching her purse as he sped past. She lost her footing on the slippery cobbles and fell.

Stunned and trying to catch her breath, she lay on the sidewalk. A group of people gathered around her.

Lydia was by her side in an instant and clutching her hand. "My friend is hurt! She's been robbed," she cried out to the onlookers.

Kate sensed a shadow looming over them. A man spoke urgently into a phone. The words were in Greek, but she knew that deep voice. She peered up at him. *Aleksei.* He gestured Lydia to stand up and move away from Kate, so he could take her place.

"Kate, it's okay. The ambulance is on its way. No, don't move." He put a restraining hand on her shoulder when she tried to get up.

Her handsome ex-boss knelt beside her, put a supporting hand behind her head.

"Are you okay? You hit the ground very hard. We need to call the police and get you checked out by a doctor."

Something wet trickled down her cheek. She swiped at it and saw blood on her hand. "I think I'm bleeding."

He brushed aside some strands of her hair and surveyed the gash on her temple. "Yes," he confirmed, "you are a little."

"Oh, dear, I seem to be making a habit of this—falling over, I mean, and bashing my head. But I'm not tipsy this time, I promise you." She made a feeble attempt at humor.

His sensual mouth quirked into a smile. "I should hope not, at this time in the morning." His eyes looked deep into hers for a moment, then he looked away at the crowd that gathered.

She heard him speak rapidly in Greek again, and some of the onlookers moved away.

Lydia's voice rang out from a distance. "Yes, I think she's okay. The police and the paramedics have been called."

Kate's eyes looked up to him again. He wore his customary white cotton shirt with sleeves rolled up. But this one was dotted with red drops. "I'm afraid I've dripped blood on you."

"What? It's not a problem." He looked again at the cut on her temple. "It looks like the bleeding has stopped. But we still need to get you looked over." He looked around. "Where is that ambulance?"

For just a few moments, she lay there and let herself relax into his steady grasp. She could see the muscles in his biceps flexing imperceptibly beneath the fine cotton of his shirt. Her eyelids began to feel heavy, and she was on the point of drifting off when the sound of a siren got louder and louder.

The ambulance attendants checked her over, then lifted

her on to a gurney and loaded her into their vehicle. The police had also arrived and were examining the scene, questioning bystanders.

Relieved the ambulance and police were finally on scene, Aleksei took a breath. He couldn't believe it when he'd seen Kate step out of the shop, then be assaulted and knocked down. He hadn't been sure about when she planned to visit Naxea while island hopping. He was only here now because Marina's baby had arrived early. If truth be told, he was so glad to have found her, even though he wished she wasn't injured like this. He'd never stopped thinking about her since they'd made love.

"You are being taken to the local hospital, where you will be examined more thoroughly," he told her. "I'll follow in my car, and I expect that the police will want to talk to you, too."

"My purse." She tried to sit up.

"Don't worry about that now," he assured her.

As the ambulance pulled away, he turned and noticed a brown paper bag lying on the cobbles. He bent over and picked it up, peeking inside to see a carton. Opening the bag, he pulled the box out. He frowned, a cold chill snaking up his back.

"Oh, that's Kate's," a blonde girl said, coming up behind him. "She'd just popped into the pharmacy to get something for her tummy. She's not been well."

"Yes, so I see," he growled as he scowled at the Greek lettering on the side of the box. "And you are?"

"Lydia, Kate's friend."

"You'd better come with me."

K ate lay on a bed in the emergency department of the island's small but modern hospital. Her head wound had
been treated, but she had stopped the doctor when he'd suggested a scan, explaining that she thought she was pregnant.
The doctor had calmly organized a test and now she was
anxiously awaiting the result. Was she really having a baby?

She wiped her sweating palms on the hospital gown
she'd been given to wear. She still couldn't get over seeing
Aleksei—what was he doing here? Okay, Naxea was his
home, but while she was still working for him, she'd known
from his diary that he wasn't due to return for his summer
visit for another two weeks. That was partly why she had
chosen to come to the island now.

Aleksei was supposed to have arrived here after she'd
left, to spend the whole of August on the island as he always
did. Only this year his stepsister would be giving birth to her
first child about halfway through the month. He had grudgingly described to Kate how he would have to be in worship-
ful attendance after what could be the entrance of the first
male Aleksanou heir…

The birth of his sister's first child. And in seven months…
Kate stared at the ceiling. What on earth was she going
to do? A finger of anxiety trailed the length of her spine.
She'd faced by a dilemma like this before. But last time she'd
been a teenage student who'd hardly known how to look
after herself, let alone a baby. She'd been frightened, lonely,

humiliated, and weak, with so much to lose, and then nature had made the choice for her. How much she had regretted that.

The memories were still as painful, seven years on, and they'd stopped her from thinking this time about what was happening, how she should handle it. For the past few weeks, she'd been living in denial...

Her thoughts were interrupted by the return of the doctor who confirmed that she was indeed pregnant. After some more checks, including a scan, he pronounced her about ten weeks along and that, yes, the baby was fine, despite her tumble. She could leave the hospital. but she needed to rest for the next couple of days and was to return immediately if she experienced pain, nausea, or bleeding. Kate was surprised by the small bounce of joy that rippled through her at the confirmation.

After Kate promised the doctor she would visit her GP as soon as she got back to London, a nurse helped Kate to her feet and then to dress. "Your friend is here to take you home," the kindly woman pronounced. She directed her to the hospital's main lobby.

But it wasn't Lydia who awaited Kate—it was Aleksei, his expression serious, accompanied by a police officer. What was this all about?

He came forward and took Kate's arm, and then he and the policeman escorted her into a private office. "I'm glad you're okay," he said, his eyes showing his concern.

She just nodded. As far as he knew, she'd had an accident, and there was nothing more to worry about. She was relieved to see him, though. His presence was strangely reassuring.

The police officer didn't speak much English, so Aleksei acted as interpreter. Kate told the officer that the scooter rider had stolen her purse, which contained her travel money, bank cards, phone, and passport. The policeman confirmed there was an immigrant gang on the island that had been preying on tourists since the start of the summer. Perhaps it was shock setting in, but she wanted to burst into tears. What *was* she going to do? She fought with herself to keep a stiff upper lip; she didn't want Aleksei to see her cry again. But she couldn't stop her eyes filling with moisture.

Aleksei put a hand on her knee and rubbed it. "I suggest I take you to my home for a few days, where you will be properly looked after and we can sort out getting you a new passport."

She wiped her eyes. His offer was very tempting, but she wasn't sure she wanted to be in such close proximity to him after the news she'd just had about the baby; she needed time to think. "That's very kind of you, but I don't want to impose on you. Perhaps you could lend me some money, and I'll be able to sort out my passport and stuff? I'll pay you back."

He gave her a small smile, but she detected a slight stiffness in him. Had she offended him?

"I think it would be best if you come with me. You need to rest and you need someone nearby if you feel unwell. Doctor's orders," he said, his voice firm.

"You spoke to the doctor?" An alarm bell rang in her head. Surely the doctor wouldn't have broken confidentiality.

"Yes. He was concerned that somebody should be with you for the next twenty-four hours to make sure you haven't got a head injury."

"Oh." Her brain whirled. He seemed calm and concerned about her fall, nothing more. Then a thought dawned on her. "Where's Lydia?"

"I've sent her back to your hotel."

"Well, I must go there, too. Lydia will look after me. I'll be fine."

"I think it would be best if you come with me," he repeated. "Kate, be reasonable. You've had a nasty experience. You need looking after," he pressed.

Her shoulders slumped. She still felt weak, and her hands kept trembling. The aftereffects of her mugging and having her pregnancy confirmed were setting in. She hadn't had any breakfast because of her morning sickness.

He must have noticed her shaky state. Standing up, he declared, "No more arguments. We're going back to my place." He said something in Greek to the police officer, who also stood up, leaned across to shake Kate's hand, and then left.

He helped her to her feet. "Come on, young lady," he said a touch more kindly, though she noticed his grip on her arm. "Let's take you home."

She submitted to being steered out of the hospital and to the parking lot. He guided her to his sleek, top-of-the-line sports car sitting under the shade of a cypress tree. He flicked the remote control, and the car's lights flickered briefly, then he yanked open the door and helped her into the passenger seat.

He strode around the hood, then got in and started the engine, but he did not put the car into gear. She found her eyes welling again with hot tears. Maybe it was her hormones, but unable to hold back the inner pressure of the last few weeks and her present feeling of distress, she bent her head into her hands. For long seconds, her shoulders heaved, and she sobbed her heart out.

After a while, he reached out and attempted to move her fingers from her tear-streaked face and encircle them with his own.

She shook him off, trying to gulp down her emotion.

He paused momentarily at her rejection, then he slid an arm around her shoulders and pulled her toward him. "You've had a horrible ordeal. Let me take care of you."

She forced herself back under control, hiccuping and wiping at her wet cheeks. She let herself lean into his warm body just a little, inhaling the comforting smell of his citrus cologne.

He continued holding her and retrieved a tissue from the glove compartment for her.

"I'm so sorry," she apologized. "I always seem to be bursting into tears on you these days. I don't normally cry this much."

"It's all right. You are in a fragile state right now. So I'm going to take you to my villa. You're staying in a flea pit and I refuse to let you remain there," he said.

"It's all…all we can afford—we're backpacking," she defended, dabbing her eyes with the tissue. "Anyway, it's not that bad. It's basic, but it's clean."

"Okay, the hotel's clean, but I will not let you stay there, certainly not while you're in this condition."

She looked up at him, and he returned her stare steadily. He couldn't know, could he, about the baby? She waited a while for the admission to come, but he said nothing.

"But what about Lydia?"

"Lydia knows where you are. I told her you'd call her tomorrow."

Kate sighed. "She's gotten used to spending evenings on her own during this trip."

"Why's that?"

"Oh, I've been a bit of a drag these last few weeks. I've been going to bed early instead of sampling the local nightlife because I've been feeling so tired and queasy…" She mentally stuffed her fist in her mouth as the admission slipped out. She waited again for him to take the cue, but still he did not respond in the way she feared.

"All the more reason for you to come to my home and relax for a couple of days. You'll have everything you need." He gave her shoulder an affectionate squeeze before releasing her. "Just sit back and relax now." With that, he swiftly fired the engine, put the car in gear, and sped off.

They traveled in silence for a while, along a winding road that took them through the narrow streets of Thira, the island's main town, past whitewashed buildings and narrow, winding alleyways and out onto the coastal road.

Kate leaned her head against the cool glass of the car window and looked out at the magnificent view of cliffs rising into a heat haze above a twinkling, sunlit aquamarine sea. In the distance she could see more charming white stone buildings, with traditional blue-painted window shutters and doors, tumbling down the hillside toward the water. On a point high above them, a church with its bell tower and small stubby spire of an Orthodox cross cast shadows on its terra cotta–tiled roof.

She thought listlessly about Aleksei's kindness and protectiveness. Hard though it was to admit, she felt like a hot mess and she was in a pickle, without her passport, phone, and money. Being able to sort herself out while staying at his home would be a relief. The hotel where she and Lydia were staying was short on creature comforts. Perhaps she could persuade Aleksei to let Lydia come and stay with him, too. And, as far as she could tell, he was none the wiser about the baby, and she would have time to work out what to do next.

His deep tones cut through her reverie. "Lydia told me how sick you've been these last few weeks."

She lifted her head and worked hard on keeping her face impassive. "Well, I haven't been *that* sick," she responded as casually as she could. "Like I said, just a bit tired and queasy. I think I must have one of those lingering tummy bugs."

He raised an eyebrow while keeping his eyes on the road. "Are you sure that's all it is? You're looking pale and washed out. Not what I would have expected after nearly ten weeks of vacation."

She hesitated. "I…I haven't been sleeping so well, and we have been traveling a lot." She knew her excuses sounded feeble.

"Did the doctor not check it out?"

"Oh…I didn't tell him."

"Ah. Then definitely I think you must stay with me and see if you can't get over your illness properly. I can arrange for my own physician to examine you."

She closed her eyes in an effort not to protest. She didn't want him to find out. Not right now.

"Kate, are you okay?"

"Yes. Look, I'm sorry. I know I'm being silly. It's just that it's all been a bit of a disappointment, being unwell like this and having to miss out on some of the things that we planned to do."

"Well, here's your chance to relax and get better, and to enjoy some real Greek hospitality at the same time," he replied cordially. "Perhaps, when you feel well again, I can show you some of the island."

She let out a relieved breath. If he was planning some sightseeing, then he couldn't be concerned about a possible pregnancy. She let some of the tension in her body go. Anyway, better to go with the flow for now, until she could get a chance to think things through properly.

At that point, the car nosed around a sharp bend on the cliff road, and an imposing set of gates came into view.

"Here we are. The Villa Aphrodite."

He stopped the car at the gates, reached into the glove compartment, and withdrew another small remote control, which he activated. He swung the vehicle through the opening gates and up a long drive shaded by olive groves and cypress trees. A large white contemporary building sat in the middle of a terrace populated by containers of flowers and palms. Kate stared in awe at its clean, sharp lines.

He pulled up in the circular area in front of the house, and immediately a boy in his late teens came out and down the front steps.

"Thanks, Dimitri." Aleksei handed the car keys to the lad, speaking to him in crisp English. "This is Miss Burrows, my personal assistant, who will be staying with us for a few days."

Kate started at his possessive description—he still thought of her as *his* personal assistant.

Dimitri rushed around to her side of the car to open the door. She got out and looked down her slightly grimy, bloodstained sundress. "I'm afraid I'm not really dressed for visiting," she ventured.

"No matter." Alexei smiled. "You will be able to bathe and change after you have been shown to your room. I have arranged for your rucksack to be collected from your hotel." He started walking toward the house.

Ushered forward by young Dimitri, Kate ascended the front steps, realizing as she went up them that they were constructed of white marble. She stared in awe as she was shown into a huge cool atrium where, at one end, an infinity pool actually entered the property. To either side of it there were glass walls running from ceiling to pool bottom, reflecting its cobalt-blue depths, which appeared to run out into the sky.

The decor was minimalist and cutting-edge, and the one dominant feature in the room was a huge canvas, painted in oils, with the same view as the one that hung in Aleksei's office in London—the small classical temple in the middle of the bay. Only this picture portrayed a vivid sunset where the sky and the reflecting sea were suffused with fiery colors.

He must have noticed her admiration for his home as he showed her the magnificent surroundings. "This place was a project that I nursed by myself," he explained proudly. "As I was building all those villas to sell and rent to other people, I saw amazing plans by many architects and decided that I could construct something bigger and better for myself. This is my private hideaway."

"It's incredible. The perfect place to come to. If I were you, I'd never want to leave."

A middle-aged Greek lady dressed traditionally in a black dress and headscarf joined them.

"Ah, here is Hestia, my housekeeper, and Dimitri's mother. She will show you to your room and look after your needs. I have some business to attend to this afternoon, but I will be back to have dinner with you here. Shall we say at seven?"

"Er...yes," she agreed, smiling to herself as she recognized Aleksei going into work mode. When they'd worked together, she'd become well aware that he could be quite focused and brisk when he wanted to get something done. She watched as he strode off along a long marble corridor to the side of the pool. No change there, then.

She followed Hestia along another corridor to the far end of the building and then up some stairs. The housekeeper opened a door into a spacious airy room that had a wall of floor-to-ceiling windows at one end.

Knowing it could be warm in the afternoons, she was grateful to feel cool air blowing on her face. He'd made sure to install air-conditioning.

Hestia went over to the windows and turned a switch, gestured as some blinds dropped down, leaving the room shaded from the midday sun. After the housekeeper had bustled around a little more to make her comfortable, she left Kate alone.

She looked around her and appreciated at once the stylish, ultramodern, light-colored furnishings, including the large bed. Her rucksack lay propped up in one corner. She went over and rummaged in it until she found her cotton robe. Then she headed for the bathroom, another spectacular affair with a walk-in shower. When she emerged, she found a tray waiting for her, with mineral water, soup, bread, and a salad of tomato, cucumber, and olives, which Hestia must have kindly brought for her. For the first time in a long time, she felt genuinely hungry. After helping herself to the food, she took her chilled glass of water and went to lie down on the bed. Sleep claimed her quickly as exhaustion set in.

When she awoke, the light behind the blinds had softened and deepened. She looked at her watch: six forty-five p.m. She stretched lazily, then got up and went over to the blinds. Turning the button as Hestia had showed her, she waited as they automatically rose to reveal a spectacular view of a small private terrace that overlooked the main terrace below with a wooden table and chairs, canvas umbrellas, teak sun beds, and the swimming pool. Beyond that, the sun lay hot on the horizon, and its rays caught the surface of the sea with sparkling fingers.

She wandered out on to her terrace, noticing pots of lavender that gave off a drowsy perfume, and then heard the chink of ice in a glass somewhere beneath her. She peered down and saw Aleksei's powerful form strolling across the lower main terrace to a far steel rail. She watched as he took a sip of his drink and, leaning against the railing, looked out across the sea, silhouetted by the rays of the dying sun. He seemed deep in thought.

She remembered that she had to get ready to join him for dinner and hurried back inside to rummage some more in her rucksack. She dug out a camisole top and long flowing skirt and put them on, surveying her reflection in a large mirror. The turquoise crinkle cotton with pretty white lace trimming looked okay against her lightly tanned skin—she had gotten some color at least. She couldn't wear a bra with this top, its straps were too thin, and she was a little taken aback to find that it felt slightly tight, as did the skirt's waistband. She'd been so sick lately, she hadn't paid attention that her breasts were fuller now. They pushed against the lacy confinement, evidence to her that she was carrying a baby.

That alarming thought brought everything back into sharp focus. She still hadn't decided what to say to Aleksei, though she knew she needed to tell him that she was having his child.

But at least the cloud of fear and denial that she'd been shrouded in for the last six weeks was clearing. As the reality of her pregnancy sank in, the paralysis that had kept her from thinking about it or dealing with it was fading away. One thing she was sure of now: she was determined to keep her baby. She just had to work out how, and the right time to let Aleksei know. How would he react?

Swiftly, she applied some light makeup, added some simple jewelry, and slid her feet into her best gold sandals. She checked her reflection again, lifting her hair up to check the head wound. Apart from the appearance of some faint bruising and, of course, butterfly tape to hold the skin together for healing, it didn't look too bad.

She made her way downstairs. Hestia waited for her in the main hall and led her out into the balmy evening air on the main terrace. Aleksei had moved to sit down at a small round table laid for dinner for two. Candles glowed, creating an intimate pool of soft light.

When he saw her standing nervously in the doorway, he stood up. The breath caught in her throat. In the descending darkness, illuminated by the candles and subtle lighting placed among the surrounding foliage on the terrace, he looked gorgeous in a green shirt and black chinos. All the feelings for him that she'd held so tight inside rushed to the surface.

She wanted him more than ever.

He also seemed unusually lost for words as he took in her appearance. For a few seconds, both stood silently, then he gestured for her to come and sit down at the table.

Carefully, she made her way across to the table, and he held a chair out for her. She sat, tried to compose herself and dispel the hot flush of need that heated her skin, glad that she could hide in the flickering candlelight.

He went to an ice bucket that contained a chilled bottle of champagne. He deftly opened it, then offered her a glass of bubbling liquid.

"I think we have something to celebrate," he suggested cheerfully.

"We do?" *What does he know?*

"Indeed. Welcome to Naxea, and to my home." He lifted his glass toward hers in a toast. She involuntarily raised the drink toward her lips but stopped short as the realization hit her that she shouldn't touch alcohol, not now that…

His eyes narrowed. "Is there something wrong with your champagne?"

"Oh…oh, n-no," she stammered and hurriedly pretend-ed to take a small sip, while she eyed a nearby terra cotta urn planted with succulents and mentally promised she would discreetly dispose of the sparkling wine as soon as she was able.

"One thing I will always remember about our work-ing together is that you always enjoyed a glass of good champagne when we entertained clients." He grinned. "Though only one glass, of course," he teased, his dark eyes crinkling with humor.

She couldn't help smiling back. "Well, someone had to stay sober and make sure that everything ran smoothly."

"You were always admirably professional and collected while doing your job. I've really missed you, just as I thought I would."

Warmth suffused her cheeks. "I'm sure Susan is taking care of you just as well as I did."

He sighed. "Susan is very organized and takes orders well. But she doesn't have your intelligence and initiative." He shook his head. "And for someone so proper and chilly in manner, she doesn't have your knack for dealing with my private life."

"Your private life?" For a moment, she couldn't figure out what he meant. The she realized what he was inferring, and laughed. "You mean that she doesn't get rid of your girlfriends?"

His smile stretched across his handsome face, and his teeth flashed white. "I think Susan disapproves thoroughly of how I pursue my relaxation. Whereas you always took it in stride."

He raised his glass to her again in salute.

She laughed again. "It's not very nice, you know, having to fend off your discarded ladies. I feel for Susan."

"And there I was thinking what a loyal assistant you were."

"I was loyal, but there were times when I could have throttled you for being so cavalier."

"Cavalier? This is an English word I do not know."

"It's derived from French, actually. It describes someone

who is offhand and devil-may-care," she informed him lightly.

He laughed. "Is that what you really think of me? That I am the devil?"

She wished she could take a gulp of her champagne. "Not *the* devil," she replied bravely. "But you can be a little bit devilish sometimes." It felt good to banter with him once more.

He raised an eyebrow, then placed his glass on the table beside him, took her hand and pulled her to her feet so that the tips of her breasts collided with his chest.

She felt her nipples tighten involuntarily.

He raised his fingers to brush away some stray curls that the warm wind blowing off the sea had thrown across her forehead.

"And you, my angel, bring out the devil in me." He raised her chin so that he could look at her directly and ran his fingers lightly across her cheek. His molten eyes searched hers before he lowered his mouth toward hers.

Her heart missed a beat as his lips brushed hers. She gasped, and he briefly slid his tongue against hers.

Now a different type of heat suffused her body.

The sound of tinkling china made her spring back and look around. Hestia and Dimitri were bearing a sumptuous dinner to serve to them.

Soon the table was groaning with local delicacies: stuffed vine leaves called *dolmathakia me rizi, piperies psites*— grilled bell peppers, baked spinach with three cheeses, cucumber and feta salad with mint, *arni a la hasapa*—baked lamb with tomatoes—and *kotopoulo lemonato*, chicken with lemon. Aleksei translated each dish's Greek name as mother and son laid them on the table and then retreated.

Delicious as it looked, Kate doubted now she could eat much of any of it, but she knew she had to try. She helped herself to small portions, nibbling on them and picking out the feta cheese—couldn't eat that now that she was pregnant.

Aleksei talked enthusiastically about the ingredients of their meal and the best way to prepare them, reminiscing how he had watched his aunt and her housekeeper cook in her large stone-flagged kitchen.

"Of course, my aunt's house had a traditional open range for cooking. I have made sure that Hestia has the most up-to-date version here."

"Kind of like an Aga," Kate suggested, thinking of the stoves that graced some English homes, and wondering why he talked about his aunt's kitchen and not his mother's.

"Similar, but with more facilities for grilling, I think."

"It's one of my ambitions to have an Aga one day," she volunteered conversationally.

"In a cozy kitchen with children playing at your feet?" he suggested softly.

She put down her fork. Suddenly she felt an overwhelming urge to confess, get her news out and over and done with.

"What is it?" he asked. "Don't you like your food? You haven't eaten much at all. Or drunk your champagne. Are you feeling unwell again? Is it your head? Does it hurt?"

The solicitousness in his tone made her tremble, but her words sat in her throat.

"I…I am feeling a bit strange. I think I need to go to my room…"

She pushed her chair away from the table with the intention of getting up, but he was quicker off the mark. He swiftly got up, walked around the table, and was behind her chair, his hands on her shoulders. She stilled, feeling the electricity of his touch, wondering what he was going to say. He caressed her upper arm. "I am well aware this isn't easy for you. But we have some unfinished business between us, issues that need to be out in the open."

Her shoulders stiffened. "I don't understand."

He continued huskily, "We have been intimate, Kate. And since that last night in London, I've thought of little else, of your lovely face, your beautiful body as it opened up to me. I want that again. I want you."

She swallowed hard as his frank words hit home, and a sensation of heat pooled in her stomach, spreading down toward her thighs.

He bent down, lifted up her hair, and trailed kisses down her neck to her sensitive nape. Almost unconsciously, she tilted her head and leaned back against him, greedy for the touch of his lips again. She had tried so hard to block out the memory of making love with him, but deep inside she still yearned for him so badly.

Slowly he turned her around and pushed back her hair from her face. "Do you want me, *pethi mou*?"

She raised her hand and trailed her fingers down his chest. Her heart pounded and her blood rushed. "Yes," she admitted in a whisper. "I do."

He pulled her toward him with his free hand. "How much do you want me," he whispered.

She breathed in, inhaling the male scent of him, letting it course through her body, arousing her and heating her. "I want you to take me to bed. *Now.*"

He looked at her with eyes heavy with desire and captured her mouth with his.

Chapter Five

His big hands cupped her breasts, his thumbs stroking back and forth. Her nipples puckered, begging for attention. She angled her body toward him.

The balmy night air danced over her heated skin. He kissed a trail down her throat, and she arched in anticipation of their arrival on her aching tips. Her breasts felt exquisitely tender and heavy as he suckled one and then the other.

Straightening, he put an arm around her waist and moved her closer to him before starting to walk both of them along the terrace. He guided them quickly to some steps that led to another upper terrace, and then along to more stairs, and high up to another level and a wooden deck-style balcony.

It seemed to Kate to take forever, but then at last he took her through some open French windows and into a dimly lit room, sweeping aside gauzy white curtains that billowed slightly in the breeze.

"Lie down," he urged, gesturing toward a large bed.

Suddenly nervous, she crossed her arms over her chest.

He removed her protective hands from her bodice. "Don't hide yourself," he coaxed as he exposed her body to his scrutiny once more.

"Your breasts are so beautiful." He knelt over her, cupped and caressed them, brushing his thumb across their stiff peaks. Then he ran his hand down her bare midriff to her skirt. She held her breath as his hand slid under her waist to find the button and unfasten it before she arched her lower back and raised her bottom slightly from the bed so that he could pull the garment away. His hands ran back up the length of her thighs to the edge of her lacy briefs before he eased them from her.

Placing his palm on the slight swell of her tummy, he stroked her there, almost possessively, for a few moments while looking down at her with heated intensity.

He moved his attention to the cleft between her thighs, slid a finger into her slick heat. She parted her legs, aching for him, welcoming his exploration. He found her bud and circled it, sending fire through her body. He slid a finger inside her, and she arched up to meet his hand, wanting him to hurry. She moaned, pushing and writhing against his skillful hand.

"Do you like it, *pethi mou*? I think you do." He positioned himself and moved his hands beneath her buttocks, raising her body to welcome him. He entered her, then stilled. "You are so hot and wet for me. I wanted to take my time with you tonight, but I—I can't."

He pulled almost all the way out, then thrust again, and again.

She groaned her need, and his mouth sought hers as

he pushed against her harder and faster now, and she felt her insides melt and flood away. She couldn't stop herself, couldn't hold back any more…

Her whimper of release stilled his movements. He angled his hips and stroked, bringing her back up again. No one else had ever given her this gift. Her whole body felt alive under his ministrations. Tingles raced through her arms and legs, and just as she exploded, he allowed his own climax to spill.

He shuddered over and over as his warm seed flooded into her. He kissed her tenderly and then rolled over, taking her into his arms.

She lay in his embrace, reveling in their closeness, the fit of their bodies, his legs tangled in hers. "Aleksei?"

There was no answer, only the sound of his rhythmic breathing. She raised her head and looked at his slumbering profile and long dark eyelashes lowered in repose. He was so, so intoxicatingly lovely.

She lay back again and exhaled. If only she could stay like this forever, here in his arms. For a long time she just drifted. Then her mind began whirring and reality began crowding back in.

She wondered what his intentions were. A quick affair while she stayed at his house and sorted out her passport and other stuff? He would have realized that she would be going home soon. This was a man who craved the thrill of the chase, the challenge of seduction, the triumph of physical possession. She doubted if he would want anything more. In fact, she just knew he wouldn't. He'd had things to do, other women to see…like Phoenix.

She went to move from his arms and get out of the bed,

thinking she might return to her own room. But even though he was asleep, Aleksei's grip tightened around her and she lay back down, glad of his strong hold. She realized that if she weren't pregnant, she might have accepted a short liaison with him, if that meant she could have a little piece of him, just for a while, and to hell with the consequences.

That revelation emboldened her and frightened her all at once. A few months ago, she wouldn't have felt able to think like this at all!

But she was having his child, and though she'd let the wanting overcome her this last time, there was no way she could sleep with him again and then just wave good-bye.

A heavy sensation weighed on her. She wouldn't make love with him anymore—she was going to have to tell him she was expecting. She couldn't pretend for much longer. He had a right to know.

What place was there for a pregnant woman or an unplanned baby in his life? How would he react to the news? Her guess was that he would be courteous and responsible, insist on making arrangements for her to return to London, where she and his baby would be kept in private comfort, and he would visit on a regular basis. But sexually he'd quickly move on to his next conquest.

Memories surfaced of when she'd been just eighteen and in her first year at university. Her throat ached as she recalled the stark way in which Oliver Temperley-Smythe had pursued her, seduced her, and then discarded her, all in the name of a stupid adolescent-boy bet. She had never allowed herself to get close to any man again...not until Aleksei.

She thought of the tiny being that now flickered inside her, and a strange sense of optimism began filling her. She could suppose that life had played another cruel trick on her. But then again, she was a different person now. Stronger, still vulnerable, but more able to take care of herself. And Aleksei was the father. She had known him long and well enough to expect that he would do the right thing for his baby. But how to come to terms with her feelings for him?

For some hours, she dozed, then lay awake again as her resolve strengthened. When dawn broke, she knew one thing she should do: tell Aleksei about the baby today. She disentangled herself from him and sat up.

Immediately a wave of nausea hit her. She looked desperately around—was there an en suite bathroom? She spotted two doors. She leaped out of bed and tried the handle of nearest one. Thank goodness! She rushed in and made for the loo, just getting to it in time before retching loudly.

As she knelt over the toilet bowl, she felt a strong warm hand on her shoulder.

"Kate? Are you ill?"

She turned her head around slightly to say something, but another bout of sickness overcame her. Aleksei scooped up her hair while she vomited.

Eventually, it stopped and she leaned her head against the cool porcelain. He bent down and wiped a washcloth soaked in cold water around her face.

"Thank you," she mumbled.

He helped her to her feet, making her aware of their nakedness. But where his body was firm and warm, hers was cold and shivering.

"Come on. We need to get you to your room and into bed."

He led her out of the bathroom and wrapped the bed's quilt around her before taking her downstairs to her own bedroom.

She crawled in bed, exhausted.

Silently, he tucked her in and stroked her forehead until she fell asleep.

D ressed casually in a polo shirt and faded jeans, Aleksei sat at the table on the main terrace. He'd just finished checking in with Susan. It was only eight thirty in London, and he'd caught her just as she arrived. He had the feeling he'd flustered her. But maybe he had been a little short with her. She was diligent and efficient, if a little slow on the uptake, and it wasn't her fault that, earlier this morning, he'd been shaken to the core.

A solitary wasp landed on the froth left on the side of his coffee cup, and he swatted it away with irritation. He looked up at the villa and his eyes went to the window of Kate's room. Finding her bent over the toilet had been a shock. The doctor would be here any minute to check her over.

Tension cramped at the back of his neck, and he raised his hand to massage the muscles. But his fingers couldn't dispel the insistent thought that hammered at his brain. *Kate really was pregnant.* She was having morning sickness. And, of course, after the hit-and-run yesterday, he'd found that test, which now was burning a hole in his back pocket.

She was having a baby—was it his? In London, it had been clear that she didn't have a boyfriend and, he had sensed, hadn't for a while. But she'd talked about having a holiday romance. He leaned his elbows on the table and rubbed his temples hard. *Christos!* Had she gotten herself knocked up by some idiot feckless backpacker?

Then a finger of guilt stabbed at him: *he* wasn't much better. He hadn't used protection on either of the occasions that he'd made love to her. He'd carelessly assumed she was on the Pill.

He sat back in his chair and surveyed the clear blue sky. What if the baby was his? Surprisingly enough, he found himself hoping it was. Partly because, he realized, he couldn't bear the thought of Kate carrying another man's child, and also because this was what he'd long wanted: a son or daughter of his own. And that Kate was the mother, well, maybe it could work out okay.

Always swift to search for answers, a solution began forming in his mind. It would require a huge change of mind-set and lifestyle for him, but, on the other hand, it was a challenge that he could get his teeth into, work at, make it yield a profit—a little like a successful company merger, of which he had achieved a number in his time. Suddenly, he felt motivated and energized. Just then, the wasp returned to try its luck again, and this time, he took his napkin and squashed the hapless insect.

The elderly doctor stood back after examining Kate while Aleksei leaned on the bedroom door frame. "The head wound is healing nicely. The vision, it is fine, Miss Burrows, and you no longer have the headache," he pronounced in heavily accented English. "That you did not do the vomit last evening tells me that you do not have the concussion."

She gave him an uneasy smile. "That's good to hear."

The doctor gave her a piercing look and then turned to Aleksei and cleared his throat. "I will talk to Miss Burrows in private, if you please."

Aleksei nodded and stepping back into the hallway, closed the bedroom door.

When the doctor had gone, Kate rose from her bed. She made her way to the window and opened the blind, blinking in the bright sunlight. She could see Aleksei out on the main terrace, surrounded by breakfast things, with his tablet and phone on the table. She chewed her bottom lip. She *had* to tell him the truth. She headed for the shower, dressed, and made her way downstairs.

When she arrived on the terrace, Aleksei was checking his phone for messages. He looked up and gestured for her to sit down. His expression looked as serious as Kate felt.

"Would you like some breakfast?"

Kate gave him a wan smile. "Some juice, yogurt, and tea would be great, thank you."

Aleksei signaled to Hestia, who had been hovering in the background, and gave the order for her breakfast.

He turned back to her. "So, what did the doctor say?"

She squared her shoulders and mustered as much composure as she could. "There's something I have to tell you."

He put down his phone and studied her carefully. "And what's that?"

"I'm pregnant."

He leaned back in his chair, and his eyes lingered on her. "I wondered when you were going to tell me."

"But you can only have guessed this morning when I was so sick!"

"Actually, I realized yesterday," he said calmly, and leaned forward to haul the slim box containing her pregnancy test out of his pocket. He placed it on the table. "You dropped this yesterday at the scene of the accident."

"Oh." She looked at the carton and flushed. "I actually did a test at the hospital. That's when I had it confirmed to me."

He placed his hands on the table and laced them together. "Were you told how far along your pregnancy is?" he asked, his brow furrowed.

"About ten weeks."

"So the child is probably mine?"

Her hackles rose. "Yes, of course it is."

He unclasped his hands and ran a thoughtful finger along the table, his eyes lowered. "I remember you telling me that you were hoping to have a holiday romance while you were here in Greece. How do I know that you didn't have a fling with some fellow tourist or a local waiter trying his luck during your first two weeks of vacation?"

Her chin rose defiantly, while inwardly she cursed herself for having used that fantasy to pretend she didn't have feelings for him. "I think you know me better than that!"

"So you haven't had a holiday romance?"

"No, I haven't. For most of the time, I've been feeling tired and queasy because I'm carrying your baby!" She heard her voice rise a couple of notches, but she didn't care at this point.

He raised his palm to her. "Okay, okay."

"Are you always this cynical?" she asked him.

He lifted an eyebrow. "Just checking the facts before I make you a proposition."

"A proposition? What do you mean?"

He exhaled heavily. "Well, neither you nor I have had time to think things through entirely, but it seems to me that there's one obvious way to deal with this situation…and that's for us to marry."

Her eyes widened. "*Marry?* You want *me* to marry *you*?" she gasped.

Chapter Six

A look of injured pride marred Aleksei's handsome features. "Is the thought of marrying me really so awful?"

Kate couldn't suppress an almost hysterical laugh. He looked kind of offended. "No!" she said quickly. "It's just that…" She took a gulp of air to steady herself. "I thought you'd want to make discreet arrangements for me and the baby. You know, move us into a suitable apartment in London, arrange visitation, come by every other Sunday to take the baby out to the park, not cramp your style."

He viewed her through narrowed eyes. "Is that what you want?"

She sighed. "To be honest, right now, I have no idea what I want. But I guess I wouldn't say no to something like that. After all, it would be hard for me to get by on my own otherwise, in a small, one-bedroom apartment in a huge, grimy city, with no job to go back to."

His expression softened. "There's no way I would allow

that to happen. I want to look after you and our child. Both of you will have everything you need if we marry."

Her head sprung up. "*Everything* we need?"

"I know that right now you deserve support, a chance to enjoy your pregnancy, and the reassurance that our child will have a loving, stable home."

Hestia arrived with Kate's breakfast, which gave her a little time to regroup and gather her thoughts.

She reluctantly ate a few spoonfuls of yogurt while Aleksei watched her, his expression hawkish. Wanting to put an end to his scrutiny, she put her spoon down and tilted her head to one side. "Okay…" she said slowly. "If we're talking about everything, what about us?"

He stretched a hand across the table, and his fingers closed over hers. She felt darts of electricity traveling from his fingertips, and her nerve endings sparked. "You cannot deny there is something special when we have sex," he said, his voice low and intense now.

She swallowed at the vision of their tangled bodies, slick with passion and exhausted by explosive lovemaking. She pushed it away. "So, if I married you, you'd expect me to be your wife in *every* sense?" she ventured tentatively.

He gave her a lazy, sexy smile. "I would."

Her stomach did a traitorous somersault. For seconds, she looked at him, taking in the full magnificence of him, and her throat felt parched. It was so tempting to believe in this dream he was laying before her. But he was Aleksei—in control, slightly paternalistic, making sure everything in his world was watertight—but he didn't know what she really needed. "Why would you want to marry a woman you don't love and who doesn't love you?" she blurted.

The question lay heavily for seconds in the air between them, and she thought she saw a shadow pass over his face. But then his expression became neutral, and he said in a matter-of-fact tone, "It's true that we don't love one another. But I want to do the right thing. We will love our baby. And you and I, we make a good team. We respect one another, and we know from working together that we are able to prioritize what matters."

That statement brought Kate right down to earth with a thud, and she withdrew from his clasp. "You make it sound as if we're going into business together."

"In a way we are," he agreed. "The business of building a family."

His logical, unemotional reply scraped at her senses. "That seems a little cold and bloodless."

He frowned. "It doesn't have to be. We may not be in love, but we can still be lovers." He looked her straight in the eye. "There will certainly be warmth in our marital bed. I would like to think that our baby will have some brothers and sisters."

"So I would be your wife in every sense…and you would be my husband in every sense?"

"That's the idea."

She hesitated. A picture arose from her memory of his phone lying on her bed in London with Phoenix Jones's text message on its screen. "You told me when we dined in London that you aren't cut out for long-term involvement. Last night, we joked about how your personal assistants need to be able to handle your girlfriends. Be honest, Aleksei, you change women more often than you change your shirts! How can you go from living the life of the carefree playboy-about-town to committed husband and father?"

His mouth curved into a wide smile. "That's a direct question and a very good one. Because I will put my mind to it, my shoulder to the wheel, and make it happen, for the sake of our child."

"In the same way you turned your family's property business into an international multimillion-pound empire?"

"There's a similarity in approach, yes," he conceded.

"Should marriage be that tough?" she observed, thinking of her own parents' happy, lasting union. "Obviously, you have to work at it. But if you're having to dig out the foundations from scratch, always calculating what to do next —"

She was struck when she looked at him now — his face had hardened, its normally fine planes and angles jutting sharply. "Maybe you have a somewhat rose-tinted view of marriage, Kate," he said flatly. "Believe me, there are many who marry for reasons other than love."

She thought about this for a moment and a lightbulb went on in her head. "I was going to say that sounds really bleak. But maybe you and I come from such different backgrounds that we have different expectations. My background is very ordinary, English suburban, while in your world, I imagine people marry to forge alliances, secure fortunes, and produce heirs."

His jaw relaxed a little, and a small smile played around his lips again. "You're perceptive. It's true that in my world, marriage is often for those reasons. But the rich and dynastic seek love and acceptance, too. Regardless, in my experience, love is but a fleeting thing and more likely to be taken than received."

Wow! She blinked at his uncompromising assessment.

She wanted to ask him why his view was so dark; what had happened to make him an unbeliever? But as if he sensed she was preparing to probe, he said, "Take your time, think it over." He still sounded as if he was coaxing her to put her signature on a contract.

"I will."

"I expect you would like to rest today." He moved smoothly on, changing the subject, something she had witnessed him do in tricky client negotiations when he had applied a certain amount of pressure then withdrawn into charm to beguile the other party and let them think they had some control in the process. "Why don't you relax on your terrace or by the pool and read? You could even go down to my private beach."

"I was thinking I really need to sort out my affairs. I should cancel my cards, get my money and passport replaced. The thieves will have emptied my bank account by now."

He waved a hand. "You will have to cancel your cards, but I will also have the police station contact your bank and confirm that you were robbed. If there are any problems, I will cover any missing funds. I will also ensure that you receive a new passport."

"Thank you." She felt a wave of gratitude. He could snap his fingers and everyone would come running. "I would like to go into Thira, too," she announced. "I want to catch up with Lydia and tell her about the baby. Perhaps I could ask her to come and stay? She must be getting fed up with being left on her own."

"Ah, yes. The flaky friend."

"Lydia's not flaky!" she protested.

"I think you might find that she's not on her own and

won't want to come here."

"What do you mean?"

"Let's just say this is a small island, and news travels fast. I think you should call her before you go traipsing into Thira. You need to rest."

L ater that afternoon, Kate sat down on the private beach under some shady pine trees, her knees pulled under her in contemplation, listening to the cicadas and watching the clear blue water of the Aegean pull gently in and out. So much had happened in the last twenty-four hours. If she needed confirmation that her life had changed forever, now she had it.

She'd called Lydia earlier, and her friend's response had borne out what Aleksei had said. Far from being abandoned and alone, Lydia had sounded surprised to hear from Kate.

"Oh, hi…hi. *Shush*, it's my mate Kate calling…" Lydia had broken off, giggling, and Kate could hear a man's voice in the background. "Sorry about that. Some local interference." Lydia had started giggling again and then given a loud squeak. "Oh! Kate, look, I'm sorry…"

"Lydia, have you got someone with you?"

"Hang on a mo… Yes!" she'd hissed in a low voice. "I've met the most gorgeous guy — Georges. Oh, Kate, he's lush!"

"So you're okay then?"

It turned out that Lydia was absolutely fine and quite happy to be with her new beau. Kate had thought about asking her to come and stay, and also about explaining her own predicament, but realized her friend wasn't really paying attention. So she'd cut the conversation short, telling Lydia that Aleksei had invited her to remain at the Villa Aphrodite for a few days. Lydia seemed fine with that.

So here she was, on this tranquil beach, in possession of a marriage proposal from the father of her baby, who had quite openly admitted that he didn't love her. And if she knew him as well as she thought she did, never would let himself do so.

For the umpteenth time, she wondered why Aleksei didn't do love or commitment. He was a conundrum. He could be kind, generous, and loyal—look how he'd helped and protected her after her leaving party and also in the last day or so, and how readily he wanted to fulfill his obligation to his child. But then he had talked about their getting married like he was rehiring her as his personal assistant.

What had made him so allergic to long-term relationships? She recalled that sticky patch in their conversation this morning when he had revealed his low opinion of marriage and his allusion to past troubles. What was it in his background that could have made him so cynical?

Although it was perhaps a case of the pot calling the kettle black, she conceded reluctantly. How long had she avoided men? Her motivation was fear of rejection, fear of not being loved. And for that very reason she couldn't marry Aleksei. That last thought startled her. Could she really marry a man who didn't love her?

She took in some deep lungfuls of sea air. So if she couldn't marry Aleksei, what should she do? Return to her plan A—ask him to support her and the baby, get a new place in London to live, find a job, organize visitation rights? That wouldn't be easy at all. He would try to keep calling the shots. And she was still infatuated with him at some level. She wasn't sure how she was going to detach herself from having feelings about him, find a way to coexist with him as they brought up their child, without wanting him or his love. She was stuck between a rock and a hard place.

Around five thirty, she unfurled her legs and stretched them; time she went back to the Villa Aphrodite. The sun was still warm, and she was glad of the hat she'd brought to shade her. She tried to unpick her crowded thoughts and work on what she was going to say to Aleksei tonight over dinner in her head as she walked along.

By eight-thirty, the sun was setting out over the ocean in a fiery collage of colors when she made her entrance onto the subtly lit main terrace to find he had already assumed his familiar position, leaning against the terrace rail and looking out to sea. Around him, sleepy crickets sang and the heady scents of jasmine, geranium, and bougainvillea permeated the air. It was so lovely and relaxing here, she reflected as she walked toward him. In other circumstances, she'd happily live on this island.

She'd dressed carefully but casually. It was getting harder to find clothes among the supply in her rucksack that fit: her waistline had definitely expanded by an inch or two, she had a little tummy, and her boobs felt full and tight. But in the gold and green chiffon blouse and cream linen drawstring pants she'd chosen, she felt comfortable and cool.

He was wearing a crisp white shirt and jeans. He turned to face her, and it struck her again how heart-stoppingly handsome he was.

His gaze assessed her as he leaned back against the rail, his arms casually folded.

"You look very elegant."

She was glad that the low-lit terrace didn't betray her heated cheeks, which had flushed with unexpected pleasure at his compliment.

"Would you like a drink?" He moved toward a side table stocked with wine, juice, and water on ice, next to plates of sliced lemons and limes.

"Just sparkling mineral water, please."

"How did you spend your afternoon?" he asked as he handed her a frosted glass of water with ice and lemon.

"I walked down to the private beach and spent some time there. It's so lovely and tranquil."

"I am glad you are resting," he replied a touch sternly, "but I hope you didn't lie out in the sun. It's very fierce at this time of year, and not a sensible thing to do when you are pregnant."

"You sound like my dad again," Kate teased him, rolling up the sleeve of her blouse to show him her still pale and freckled arm, then realizing there probably wasn't enough light for him to tell. "I wore a hat and applied some sunscreen. I'm way too pale to risk too much exposure."

"Yes, I know just how pale you are...all over."

Heat blossomed in her chest and rose up to her face.

He laughed and opened his mouth, but his attention was broken by the arrival of Hestia and her son bearing a dinner of pita bread, aubergine and *tzatziki* dips, fresh fish, rice, salad, and fruit, which they placed on the candlelit table.

They ate the delicious food in silence for a while until Kate, drawing in a deep gulp of oxygen to give her courage, seized her moment.

"Look, I've had a chance to think things over."

He looked up from his plate and listened in inscrutable silence, his right eyebrow slightly raised.

She plowed on with what she'd rehearsed in her head. "I want the best for our baby, just as you do, and for that reason, I've decided not to marry you. I can't marry a man who doesn't love me."

He didn't say anything for a few seconds. She watched as his nostrils flared imperceptibly. But then he said coolly, "What *do* you want to do?"

"I was hoping that we might come to some kind of financial arrangement. I would like to ask for your help in finding a suitable apartment or house in which to bring up our baby in London, also with arranging child care if I need it, and working out visitation for you."

"Ah. So you want me to keep you and pay for strangers to look after our baby?"

"I'd hope we can find a really good, trustworthy nanny. I'm also hoping to get back to work after a few months so I can contribute, too," Kate volunteered, noticing his glowering expression. He wasn't pleased with her decision.

"You seem to have this all planned out," he said crisply. "What if I tell you that I have plans, too? I am working to appoint new managing directors to look after the business in London and Athens, so I can relocate to Naxea."

Kate looked at him out of the corner of her eye, feeling knocked sideways. Where had this come from?

"So I would be making flying visits to the UK only every two or three months. In which case, because I very much want to be a good father and present in my child's life, I think we shall have to get our lawyers talking about arrangements for him or her to spend periods of time with me here in Greece."

"Lawyers? I was hoping we didn't have to get them involved."

"If you intend to live on your own with our child in London, then I must insist on joint custody arrangements being made."

She blinked. She'd known he'd push back, but she felt like a mouse that had been cornered by a bird of prey. She swallowed, trying to calm her nerves. "Surely we can come to an agreement between ourselves."

He smiled, his eyes hooded in the candlelight. "I'm sure you wouldn't want our child to be subjected to the whims of something undocumented and not witnessed. Doesn't he or she deserve a life untroubled by wrangling or disagreements?" He fixed her with a stare. "It's reasonable to expect that, in time, you'll find yourself a partner, and if there are no legal boundaries in place, what would happen to our child?"

"I don't think that will happen," she said, her voice faltering.

"Oh, come on, Kate," he said silkily. "You are young and beautiful. Sooner or later, you will meet your mate."

"I've no intention of *meeting my mate*, as you put it," she said tersely. "*You're* more likely to have another woman on your arm in next to no time."

Aleksei threw back his head and laughed. His eyes rested on her. "If you won't marry me, then I may be forced to seek my comforts elsewhere."

"Well, you'd better start looking, then!" She leaped up and threw her napkin down on the table in frustration. He was impossible, always one step ahead! And she could kick herself for biting back with those last couple of remarks;

she'd wanted to tell him that their physical relationship was over in a reasonable way. Though, try as she might not to, she *hated* the thought him making love to someone else, someone who wasn't her.

Waves of some strong emotion she couldn't quite identify or control rolled through her blood. This hadn't gone well, or the way she'd planned. She felt shocked by her strength of feeling and realized she needed time to calm down, regroup, alone.

"I'm tired," she announced. "I'm going to bed. Good night." Turning her back on him, she stiffened her spine and, biting her turmoil back down, walked away with as much dignity as she could muster.

Chapter Seven

The sun was rising over the azure sea. Through the silvery morning mist that hung on the horizon, Aleksei could make out the coastline of the neighboring island of Paxanthia. He sat on his private terrace in the cold light of dawn.

Last night's conversation with Kate sat like a monkey on his back. It had been a long time since a relationship conversation with a woman had made such an impact on him. He'd become expert at batting away female emotions or any uncomfortable feelings on his part. Certainly since Aella.

Her name meant "whirlwind." He smiled a bitter smile. His ex-wife had definitely been that. She'd ripped through his life like a tornado, felling him with her beauty, passion, and fieriness. He'd been desperate to marry her, to tame her, but like all storms, she hadn't lasted long and had left a trail of havoc and destruction in her wake. When he put Aella together with the loss of his mother's love, and a childhood and adolescence watching his father being kicked around like a soccer ball by Charlotte, his stepmother, he had come to the conclusion that women were not to be indulged or trusted, and marriage for love was not to be relied upon.

With hindsight, he realized that Kate had gotten angry and stomped off because she'd been puzzled, hurt, and feeling conflicted about his marriage proposal and his dismissal of her own plans. But she'd thrown him off-kilter with her talk about financial support—too many times had he seen or experienced women greedy for what they could get—and it was almost a reflex with him to become suspicious and guarded.

He sighed heavily. His defensiveness had been wrong. He knew very well that Kate was not that sort of person. It would have been more likely that, if he'd declared undying love for her, she'd have accepted his proposal, wouldn't she? Well, apart from the fact that he told himself that he never would—though he respected her and wanted her, just like he'd told her—he got the feeling that the lack of love was just one obstacle for her, and there was something more that held her aloof.

And, like any business deal that was hard to nail down, her reluctance had made him all the keener to get a result, and he had laid out his terms tactically. Altogether, it hadn't been the best way to proceed, especially when this was a time when she must be feeling vulnerable…

Just then, he heard the faint sounds of someone retching in another part of the villa. Poor Kate! She obviously had morning sickness again. He sat for a while longer, but when the wretched noises continued, he got up and made his way along to the kitchen. Hestia and Dimitri hadn't yet arrived to start work, so perhaps he could knock up a couple of things that would help her feel better.

Kate was lying on her bed with a cold washcloth on her forehead, feeling wrung out. The nausea had passed. She heard a knock on her door. Was Hestia here already?

"Come in," she said weakly and was surprised when Aleksei entered, bearing a tray.

"I've brought you some tea and dry toast. My stepsister Marina told me that this worked for her in early pregnancy."

"Thank you!" She struggled to sit up on the well-sprung mattress, amazed. "Has Hestia arrived?"

He shook his head and smiled. "No, not yet. It's only six a.m. She and Dimitri won't be here until seven."

Her eyes opened wide. "So you made this for me?"

"Yes, it's all my own work. I could hear that you weren't well."

"Oh, no, did I wake you up?"

"I was awake already," he assured her. "Actually, I believe Marina drank ginger tea, but I couldn't find any. I'll ask Hestia to get some fresh ginger when she next goes to the market."

"Thank you," she said again. As she took the tray from him, she became aware that her thin nightgown was pulled taut and his eyes had wandered to her breasts, the outlines of which were visible through the filmy material. They were heavier now, engorging with pregnancy, the areolae darkening. She felt her nipples tighten under his scrutiny and her sex moisten. She bent her head and distracted herself by sipping her tea.

"Marina and her husband are coming to lunch today with their new daughter, along with my other stepsister, Eleni." He spoke, dragging her attention back to the present. "I'd like you to meet them and share the meal with us."

"Fine. Have you told your family about my pregnancy?"

He shook his head and said gently, "I haven't, because I wanted to discuss things with you first. But I think news may have already reached them. Hestia likes to gossip."

"Oh."

"I wouldn't worry. Everyone is besotted with Athena right now."

"Didn't you tell me that Marina thought she was having a boy?"

He raised both eyebrows. "She did. That's what she was told at one of her scans. But apparently they aren't 100 percent accurate."

Kate thought for a few seconds. "But it would be quite something if we were to have a boy?" she ventured.

His lips quirked spontaneously. "I'll be happy whatever the sex, *pethi mou*," he said quietly.

She looked at him from under her lashes, silently pleased by his response. "I thought you might be a typical Greek male," she teased, "wanting a boy child to carry on the Aleksanou dynasty."

He shrugged. "I can't deny that a son would be advantageous from a business point of view." He stopped, and she swore she saw a light shining in his eyes. "But to have a child of my own of either sex would be the most precious thing in the world."

In that moment, she knew she'd witnessed an entirely

unguarded emotion in him, and her breath caught in her throat. She hadn't known how much he wanted to have a child, and it touched something deep inside her. She touched his hand. "Thanks for sharing that with me."

He grimaced. "I've never revealed it to another human being."

"Why don't you tell Marina, her husband, and Eleni the good news about our baby today," she suggested gently. "Meanwhile, I'd better get on with trying some of that toast." She gave him a wry grin. "If I didn't know better, I'd think that you were trying to get round me."

Around lunchtime, she joined Aleksei and his family in a large open-plan living area that fanned out from the far end of the main atrium. Marina, Alexei's younger stepsister, a petite and very pretty brunette with big, calm blue eyes, sat perched on one of the large cream sofas next to her young, handsome husband, both looking happily on while Aleksei, who sat opposite them, cradled his new niece lovingly in his arms. When the baby stretched out her hand toward her uncle, Kate watched as Aleksei lowered her on to his lap and continued to cradle her with one arm while he moved his free hand toward her and let her fasten her tiny fingers around his much larger one, murmuring tender endearments.

When he became aware of Kate's presence, he scooped the baby back up into his arms and stood up.

"Kate, let me introduce you to my sister Marina and her husband, Adrastos. And my other sister, Eleni."

Kate shook hands warmly with Marina and Adrastos. Eleni, a waiflike teenage girl with a tangle of dark curly hair and eyes as equally blue as Marina's, though hers were wild and defiant-looking, stood with her hands tucked awkwardly under her armpits. Kate smiled cordially at her but got no response.

"And this is Athena." Aleksei stepped forward and lowered his arms so that Kate could get a better look at the baby girl.

Kate wasn't able to help smiling. She took small steps forward. "She's beautiful."

"Isn't she? Would you like to hold her?"

Kate looked for permission to Marina, who waved her hand in a friendly gesture of assent, and carefully Aleksei handed over the precious newborn.

For some moments, Athena looked up at her with unfocused eyes, moving her fragile limbs and puckering up her rosebud mouth with little gasps and hiccups. Kate felt her heart swell.

"She's so tiny," she managed to say.

"She was premature," Marina explained in perfect English. "But she was in good shape when she arrived and they let us out of hospital a couple of days ago, once they were happy with her breathing and feeding. This visit to her proud uncle is her first outing."

Kate spontaneously looked up at Aleksei and smiled shyly. His eyes met hers searchingly for a moment, and she felt her breath catch as he stepped closer to her and slid an arm around her shoulder.

"Also a proud father-to-be," he announced to his sisters and brother-in-law. "Kate is expecting my child."

For a moment, Marina and Adrastos looked stunned, then the latter jumped up and went to clap Aleksei on the back, causing Athena to break into a burst of wails. Marina quickly got up and relieved Kate of her crying daughter. Eleni, however, hung back and Kate thought she saw a forlorn look shadow the girl's face.

The rest of the visit passed pleasantly. After Aleksei's announcement, Marina and Adrastos seemed genuinely delighted and talked to Kate warmly. She was surprised to find that they knew a good deal about her already.

She also learned some more about the tangled Aleksanou family setup over lunch under huge shady canvas umbrellas out on the main terrace. Marina and Eleni were the daughters of Alexei's father, Theo, and his second wife, Charlotte, an Anglo-French ex-actress. It seemed that since Theo's death five years ago, Charlotte had spent most of her time living in Paris. It struck Kate that this must have been hard on Eleni, who had stayed on Naxea with her aunt Dafnia, Theo's sister, when she was home from boarding school. Certainly, Eleni said very little and scowled whenever her mother's name was mentioned.

And what had happened to Aleksei's mother? Had she remarried, and did he keep in touch with her? Kate made a mental note to ask him another time.

The visitors left late afternoon. As Aleksei escorted them to the door and Hestia cleared away the lunch things, Kate, having said her good-byes, donned her sunglasses and went to sit by the pool. It was cooler now, and she was feeling a little tired. Aleksei came out again and, spotting her, pulled up a sunbed next to her, sitting on it sideways.

"You were a hit with my sisters and Adrastos. They

really took to you. And they're delighted about our baby."

"I'm not sure Eleni was so keen to meet me," she said cautiously.

He sighed and laced his fingers together. "Don't take it personally. Eleni is a troubled girl. You might have gathered that her mother is not very interested in her." His voice grew scathing. "Charlotte was hoping for boy children when she lured my father into marriage. When Marina was born—she's twenty-seven—Charlotte was bitterly disappointed and vowed to have no more babies. But she slipped up and, ten years later, conceived Eleni accidentally. During that pregnancy her hopes rose again that she was having a boy, who would be her trump card in controlling my father and the family's fortune, but it was not to be. She practically abandoned Eleni at birth, and if it hadn't been for my aunt Dafnia, Eleni would have received no maternal love at all. I think she feels the rejection very keenly."

"You don't sound as if you have a very high opinion of Charlotte," Kate observed, watching a kind of raw anger suffuse his handsome, masculine features.

"I don't. Charlotte is the kind of woman I despise—beautiful, selfish, greedy, and cold. She exploited my father's weaknesses, spent his money, and destroyed him with numerous sexual betrayals, and she had little time or love for her daughters. Eleni has suffered greatly because of her. She certainly had no time for me when I was growing up and made sure that my father didn't, either."

She said nothing as he visibly struggled to bring warring emotions in himself back under control. She had never seen him so affected; clearly it ran deep. She was just about to ask him what had happened to his mother when he rose abruptly from the sunbed.

"I've got some work to do this evening. There's a transatlantic call coming through from New York that I will be taking. Do you mind dining alone?"

"N-no," she replied, a little startled.

"Do you have any plans for tomorrow?"

"I was hoping to make that trip into Thira. Apart from anything, I need to get some bigger clothes."

"How about I take you and we have some lunch?" he offered. "I can show you around town, and we can talk some more. I've had some more thoughts on how we might resolve our issues."

"Lunch sounds good," she accepted. She peered at him over her sunnies. "I'm not so sure about resolving our issues. Does that mean you're going to try and twist my arm about getting married?"

He quirked a brow and speared her with his gaze. "Just wait and see," he said cryptically.

"That one looks like a tent," Kate exclaimed when Aleksei held up a billowing, highly patterned maternity dress in a ladies' apparel store on the main street in Thira. He'd already taken her to a high-end store full of designer labels and eye-wateringly expensive leather and perfumes. She'd bought a beautiful dress there that would be suitable for a posh evening do: cut in a Grecian style, with a low, crossover neckline, its creamy gold material draped becomingly from a gathering just under the bust to just below the knee; it would nicely cover a pregnancy bump and make the most of her increasing cleavage. However, she wondered when she would ever have occasion to wear it.

"You insisted on coming in here," he said wearily, looking around at the simple, everyday cotton clothing.

"I just wanted some ordinary stuff. I'm going to be a pregnant whale of a woman soon, not a supermodel." She closed her eyes and bit her lip as soon as it was out of her mouth. What had possessed her to say that to him?

He shrugged, apparently unconcerned by her remark. "I'm sure you'll look as beautiful then as you do now."

"Flattery will get you everywhere."

His eyes slipped over her blossoming body. "I mean it," he said softly.

Just for a mad moment, she wanted to throw her arms around his neck and hug him for his lovely remark. But instead she smiled appreciatively and busied herself with swishing through the hangers on the carousel of maternity clothes.

He put the floral tent back on the rack. "I don't think I've got what it takes to be your personal shopper. Look, I've got some banking to do. The bank's just up the street. Why don't you select what you want, try it on, and I'll be back in about ten minutes to pay."

She laughed. "Quitter! Okay, that sounds like a plan."

Left to her own devices, she quickly picked out a couple of summer frocks, some T-shirts and cutoff pants with nice, flexible waistbands, and a cotton-knit cardigan for the evenings. As she tried them on, she was distracted by thoughts of how much more Aleksei had showed of himself in the last forty-eight hours, and how that was changing her opinion, her feelings—his kindness in bringing her to his home, making breakfast for her today, and now this shopping trip—how his eyes had shined when he talked about wanting a child, and how tender and proud he'd been with little Athena. He would be a great hands-on dad. He so wanted and *needed* to be a dad.

She'd also witnessed his anger and sadness at the divisions in his family, which had made her realize that being a father would change a great deal for him on that score. Could she really deny him the chance to heal and be happy, which she might do if she relegated him to part-time fatherhood?

She stared at herself in the changing room mirror. Their conversation yesterday evening had ended badly, but since then she'd had time to reflect and now grudgingly admitted she could see the practicality in what he'd said: it wouldn't be good for their child if they were constantly wrangling, and she dreaded the prospect of having to undergo legal mediation. She had no doubt that Aleksei would be tough in getting what he wanted; it was what he did best.

She wanted to do what was right for her baby, too. Her own family would provide help and love, and she'd never deny Aleksei access to his child. But did she really *want* to be a single mother? It niggled away at her that she wouldn't be allowing their son or daughter the everyday presence of a father like she'd had; how might the child feel in twenty years' time—would they blame her for turning the chance of marriage to their dad down?

Aleksei's comments about their baby having siblings rankled, too. She was an only child herself, had longed for brothers and sisters, and going it alone would surely ensure that her child's growing years would be as solitary as her own had been. She just couldn't see herself having another relationship.

Another relationship. An intriguing thought struck her then: in a matter of months, she'd gone from nursing an un-requited attraction to Aleksei to expecting his child and con-templating marriage, and they had a relationship *of sorts* — they'd worked together as a perfect team for two years, en-joyed each other's company, and they'd been involved sexu-ally. That last part made her insides fizz; his lovemaking had her hooked and losing it would be hard to bear — as would thinking of him giving it to another woman. All of that had to count for something, didn't it?

It was just those brick walls that they both had built around themselves to keep out any unwanted emotional in-volvement that kept them apart. Perhaps, with time, even those could be scaled…

"Kate, how are you getting on?" Aleksei's deep tones outside the changing room cut through her ruminations.

"I'm good!" she called back. "I've found what I wanted."

With the garments bought and paid for, they made their way up a side street to a charming tavern with an outside ve-randa, where they could sit under the shade of vines and lis-ten to sweetly singing birds while they ate lunch. Kate chose griddled chicken with quinoa and a Greek salad tossed in a lemon and olive oil dressing, minus feta cheese. Aleksei opted for the same, but with feta in his salad.

They chatted for a while, and then Aleksei put down his cutlery on his half-eaten plate of food with a clatter.

"Kate, I've had a chance to mull over our conversation last night. I think that maybe I was a bit hard on you."

She stopped forking food into her mouth and looked at him, her eyes wide. "You do?"

"Yes. I was approaching our conversation like a business negotiation, when in fact we are talking about our child's future…and yours. It's important that our baby has a happy mother…that you are happy." He was choosing his words carefully, and she noticed his brows knotted together in that way they had of doing when he was on unsteady ground.

She laid down her fork, too, and sat back in her chair, stunned. "Well…yes, I suppose that's true…" She looked at him inquiringly.

"I've got a new proposition to put to you…a compromise, which might suit you better, and which answers some of my concerns." He paused. "How would you feel about living here on Naxea with our baby in a place of your own?"

She was totally startled. "You mean…live here, but without us being married?"

"Yes." He nodded his head. "A house of your choice, with a nanny and a housekeeper to support you, and any other staff you feel you might need."

"Oh." The offer had come out of left field, and she was temporarily at a loss for an answer, so far was it from what he'd talked about previously.

"You'd have enough bedrooms for friends and family to come and visit whenever you pleased. You haven't told me much about your parents, but I realize you are very close to them. And I'm sure we could arrange for regular trips to England, too."

"Right. Well…um…this is unexpected!" She unconsciously pushed a stray lock of hair behind her ear, intrigued by what he was saying.

"We would still have to get a legal agreement drawn up by my lawyers, but I would make sure that all your requirements are included, and if you think of anything you need or want farther down the line, then that can be added in, too."

Wow! She met his eyes and noted that he looked sort of eager...almost boyish, as if he was unsure if his idea would get a favorable reception from her, which made her insides melt. He was trying hard to see things from her point of view, to offer her something that would work for her. Oh, crikey, she needed to think! She rose abruptly from her seat. "Sorry, just need to take a bathroom break. Being pregnant makes me want to pee continually."

With that, she rushed inside the restaurant and locked herself in the very clean restroom. She'd reached the moment of truth. Should she follow her head and accept Aleksei's latest offer, or her heart and accept his proposal? A memory of when she and Lydia had been sharing their curry on their very last night in London popped into her head. What had Lydia said? *Sometimes it's best not to overthink everything and just follow your heart...* She'd been overthinking for England! All of a sudden, something inside of her took over, drove her and compelled her...

When she returned to their table, Aleksei stood up, looking concerned. "Are you all right, Kate?"

"Yes, I'm fine," she said brightly, "thank you for your concern. That was a very generous offer you made me," she continued before he had time to reply, "and it sounds very attractive. I appreciate it." She paused and swallowed. "It's funny, but I've been thinking, too. Perhaps I've been too keen to go it alone..."

Aleksei raised an eyebrow in surprise, but then his expression relaxed a little as he listened in silence to what she had to say.

"I want the best for our baby, just as you do. It would be wrong of me to prevent him or her having the best of everything, to deny the chance of having your love on a daily basis, or of having brothers and sisters. I was an only child, and I longed for siblings." She halted again and smiled at him, then reached out to entwine her fingers with his. "I saw you with your niece, and I know that you will love our child to bits—even if you don't love me. And what you said just now…about offering me a place of my own. That was really thoughtful of you, Aleksei." She felt the pressure rise in her throat. "You know, if I'm going to be here and we're going to be cooperating so closely, well…I….we might as well get married." She leaned back in her chair a little, and her heart thumped nineteen to the dozen.

His features softened even more, and she felt him lean forward and his fingers tighten around hers.

"I think we can be a good team," she continued, her confidence increasing. "We've worked well together and closely in the past, we have things in common, and I enjoy your company…and when we make love." She knew she was blushing when she said that last bit. "We know how to play to one another's strengths. It won't be entirely easy, but we can work at it."

His face cracked into a huge smile. He disentangled himself from her grip and took his wineglass, then raised it toward her. "*Stin oraia zoe.* To the beautiful life."

"To the beautiful life." Kate clinked her glass of juice against his, dizzy from what she'd just committed herself to.

"Unfortunately, this will mean more shopping."

She blinked. "It will?"

"We must think about your wedding gown. Marina will help you. She knows every dressmaker on the island."

That stopped Kate in her tracks. "You mean a proper white wedding? I'd envisaged a quiet affair, exchanging vows in a civil ceremony at the local town hall."

"But of course. We will be married at the church that my family attend, and where my sisters and I were christened. We'll fly your parents over. I might even tolerate having that flaky friend of yours as a bridesmaid!"

Chapter Eight

Five weeks later, on the morning of her wedding day, Kate reflected on the whirlwind of new faces, places, and activities that had swept her up now that her life with Aleksei had really begun.

As Marina and Lydia fussed around her, adding the final touches to her hair and makeup, she looked at her reflection in the mirror. Her morning sickness had passed, and her face had filled out again. Her dress was stunning: of cream silk and styled in a flattering empire line to hide her small bump, it had a bodice decorated with tiny seed pearls, a low neck, and long delicate chiffon sleeves that caught at her wrists; long, soft folds of material flared out from pin tucks under her bust to pool at her feet, which were encased in pretty cream silk ballet pumps. Her auburn hair was caught up and held—Grecian style—by cream silk ribbons studded with more pearls. At her throat lay a row of small sparkling emeralds set in gold, which Aleksei had presented to her yesterday evening along with tiny emerald-and-gold drop earrings as a wedding gift to match her emerald engagement ring. Behind her she could see her bouquet of cream roses laid carefully on a chair.

In less than two hours, she would be Mrs. Aleksei Aleksanou.

"You look absolutely fabulous." Lydia's admiring voice cut into her reverie. Her friend looked very fetching herself in a simple dusky-pink dress with a pink faux silk rose in her blonde hair. Lydia had been over the moon to have the chance to return to Naxea almost exactly a month after she'd left the island, leaving a forlorn Georges behind her. In fact, the minute she'd accepted Kate's invitation to be her bridesmaid, Lydia had handed in her notice to her employers in London. She was, she announced, coming back to see if she and Georges really were the real thing, and she'd find a job in a bar. Kate was delighted to have her close by again.

She'd also found a supporter in Marina, too. Alexei's stepsister had been generous and kind in helping Kate to settle in. She had helped Kate get to know the family, including Dafnia, who, with her late husband, had been rocks in Aleksei's young life after the death of Isadora, his mother. Kate had been quite taken aback by this news. When she'd tried asking Aleksei about Isadora, he had been unforthcoming. "My mother died when I was small," he'd explained tersely, and then he'd turned their conversation to something completely different.

During the past few weeks, he had been away on business a lot, mainly, he said, tying up the loose ends of relocating to Greece. It meant that there had been little opportunity for intimacy between them, which Kate missed. She relished their lovemaking and lying safe and warm in his arms afterward. But there was plenty to keep her busy too; when Aleksei was not around, her days had been filled with the wedding arrangements.

She'd been very disappointed, though, when he hadn't been around the previous week to accompany to her scan by the obstetrician he'd had specially flown in from Athens. Marina had kindly driven her to the hospital but had tactfully waited outside while Kate had had the ultrasound. She hadn't been prepared for how her heart had filled with love when she had seen the baby gently moving on the screen. She'd felt sadness, too, because Aleksei wasn't able to be there and share this special moment with her.

But when she'd returned to the house, she'd left the small black-and-white image that she'd been given by the hospital on the desk in Aleksei's study, ready for his return. Late one evening, after he'd come home, she'd passed by the room and had caught a glimpse of him holding the scan of his tiny baby, a look of tenderness and joy on his handsome face, and once again she'd seen how much he wanted this child. That alone was enough to reinforce her courage that she was taking the right step in getting married.

"Do not look so solemn, Kate!" Marina chided her gently, bringing her back to earth. "This will be the happiest day of your life."

"Oh…yes, sorry. It's just that…I'm feeling a little nervous."

"Wedding jitters," Lydia pronounced.

"Ah, I remember them well when I married my Adrastos. I was shaking as I walked up the aisle," Marina laughed. "But you know, as soon as Adrastos turned around and our eyes met, I knew that everything was going to be okay and that I was the happiest woman in the world. It will be the same for you, Kate," she added reassuringly. "Aleksei is a good man."

"Yes, he is," Kate agreed. She summoned a smile and gathered up her dress. "Come on, get me to the church on time, ladies."

As the three women made to leave, Kate felt a hand squeezing her arm behind her bouquet and heard Lydia whisper in her ear, "You go, girl. You can win him round, you see if you don't."

Kate placed a hand over her friend's and squeezed it back. "I'm going to try."

The small white stone Orthodox church on the outskirts of Thira sat high on a steep hillside, above intricately linked whitewashed buildings that seemed as if they were tumbling down to the sea. As she stepped from the car, a gentle salty breeze disturbed a tendril of her auburn air from its confinement of plaited ribbons and pearls.

Lydia caught up the train of her dress, and Kate carefully positioned her rose bouquet in front of her. Together they walked up the church steps. Her father was waiting proudly to give her away—her parents had received the news of her pregnancy and impending marriage with a little shock and then delight; even her normally very straitlaced grandma had managed to ignore that she'd gotten pregnant out of wedlock, instead impressed that her granddaughter's husband-to-be was one of the richest men in Europe.

As she walked down the aisle of the church, its interior glowed golden with candlelight and bars of mid-August sunlight that reached in through small mullioned windows. The air was heavy with the scent of flowers. For a moment, her step faltered as she caught sight of Aleksei's broad back, his shoulders stiff as he faced the altar. Then he turned and caught sight of her. He surveyed her with a stare that set her on fire, then his eyebrows slowly raised themselves in appreciation and a half smile played around his lips. As she joined him, he stepped forward, his hand outstretched, and bent to kiss her on the cheek. As he straightened, she heard him say, "You are so beautiful."

The traditional, charming ceremony with exchanging of crowns passed in a blur. She was aware of him smiling at her throughout, quietly prompting her and whispering words of encouragement. Then it was done, and they were married. Again, he stooped to kiss his new bride, this time full on the mouth. She gasped a little as she felt his tongue probe her lips and his hands snake around her waist. The congregation clapped their happiness.

When they parted from the embrace, he continued to hold her tight, searching her face as he looked down at her. His fingers rose to touch her cheek, and she felt the electric charge of her body's recognition.

"My beautiful wife," he murmured.

Outside the church, the mood was high as Kate and Aleksei stood on the steps, surrounded by guests and well-wishers. He continued to keep her close, giving her small kisses, his arm possessively around her, and she reveled in heady feelings of warmth and affection.

The wedding breakfast was actually a sumptuous buffet lunch back at the villa. As she mingled with the guests on the terrace, Kate became aware of a small commotion: Eleni had been dragged out from behind a large ornamental rock in the garden area beyond the swimming pool. She caught sight of the teenage girl with her flushed face and wild, angry eyes as her aunt chided her for some misdemeanor. Charlotte had not come to the wedding, saying rather rudely that she had a more pressing engagement in the South of France to attend.

Lydia came up behind her and muttered in her ear, "They've got a right one there. Apparently, she was sat behind the rock smoking a joint. Georges says she's known all over the island as crazy and out of control."

Kate didn't reply, instead taking in Eleni's jerky, panicked body language as Dafnia, leaning on her cane, pulled the girl reluctantly back to the party throng. Eleni reminded her of a pretty, untamed colt. Then she saw Aleksei go over and intervene, putting a soothing hand on the twitchy girl's shoulders, talking persuasively to her in a low voice as he steered her into the villa and away from prying eyes.

Kate gathered her skirts, hurried over to Dafnia, and asked, "Is Eleni okay? Is there anything I can do to help?"

Dafnia smiled gratefully and took her hand to pat it. "Do not trouble yourself on your wedding day, my dear. Aleksei is taking care of his little sister."

Kate nodded. Eleni was clearly going through a very difficult time, and it was her family's way to gather around her to safeguard her.

The sun was setting low over the sea when the last of the guests left. As a retinue of hired caterers and cleaners set to work clearing the debris of the reception, Kate took off her pumps and decided to walk down to the beach, carrying the billowing skirts of her gown draped over her arm.

When she reached the water's edge, she used her free hand to unleash her hair from its confining ribbons and pearls and shake it out. The sea felt cool as it lapped around her ankles and soothed her tired feet. For a while, she just stood and stared out to the horizon, where she could make out the hazy purple outline of another island silhouetted against the vivid sky.

She nearly jumped out of her skin when Aleksei's arm came about her waist from behind and his lips landed on the back of her neck.

"Did I surprise you, *pethi mou*?"

"I—I was just enjoying the sunset."

"It will be dark soon. You should come back to the house." He nuzzled her neck again and she leaned back against him, shivering as his arms went around her and one hand cupped and kneaded her breast.

"Does my wife like having her neck kissed?"

"Mmm." She arched her back as his hands found her erect, excited nipples pushing at the material of her bodice.

"Your nipples have gotten so sensitive," he whispered, his tongue exploring her ear. She felt herself drowning in the waves of desire engulfing her aroused body. She shut her eyes and writhed in his hold, his hardness detectable to her even through the silk of her dress. Before she knew it, he had turned her and picked her up in his arms. She had to clasp her hands around his neck to steady herself and looked down helplessly as her hem trailed on the sea's surface.

"My dress!"

"Forget it…" He silenced her bubbling protest with a long, deep kiss.

"Oh, God, Aleksei…"

She opened her lips and welcomed his tongue. Fused together, he carried her a little way up the beach to where the sand pillowed into soft dunes and laid her down gently.

He knelt over her, shaking off his jacket and tie, unbuttoning his shirt halfway. Lowering himself beside her, he placed his hand on her gently swelling stomach, caressing her. She looked up at him and saw his fathomless dark eyes, heavy-lidded with desire.

"I desire you so much, it's been too long," he murmured before leaning down to capture her mouth again in a scorching possession.

She pulled him to her, and his lips brushed hers. She melted inside.

"You are my wife," he breathed, "and I am your husband. That is all that matters now."

Her hands rose as if controlled by some alien force to tangle in his hair, pulling him closer to her.

He unclipped the delicate emerald necklace and slid her bodice off her shoulder, enough for him to release her breast from the lacy confinement. He bent over her, licked her nipple, swirled his tongue all around it.

She arched up, clasping his head to her.

He suckled it, and she thought she'd died and gone to heaven. He felt exquisite against her swollen skin, and she arched even more, offering herself to him.

He raised his head and lifted her slightly so that he could undo the pearl buttons down the back of her dress before laying her down again and exposing her breasts entirely for his ravishment. She watched, mesmerized, as he paused for a moment to take in the ripe orbs and their taut nipples, reveling in the fire and wanting that burned in his eyes, then gasped in painful pleasure when he took one of those tender points in his teeth and nipped it. At the same time, his hand reached down and flipped up the material of her dress, then swiftly found the moist core of her, slipping inside her panties to insistently stroke her wetness and make her gasp again.

"Aleksei…" She needed him so much, needed him to be inside her.

Quickly he removed his pants, then knelt and positioned himself between her legs, wrapping them around him and raising her bottom onto his knees. He pushed his length into her and began easing backward and forward, filling her, reaching deep into her, then slowly withdrawing, making her whimper.

With each long penetration, she felt herself climbing higher and higher and then, suddenly, his rhythm changed, plunging into her with quick, hard thrusts that pushed her to the edge of ecstasy and over…

She heard his hoarse cry as he climaxed, too, saw him throw back his head as he came.

Then he retreated from her body and lay down beside her once more, pulling her to him. She buried her head against his bare chest, her fingers tracing the whorls of hair as she came back down to earth, and he gently rubbed her back and buried his lips in her hair.

They lay in each other's arms for countless minutes in the moonlight, Kate only aware of the gentle lapping of the sea at the shoreline and the sense of safety she felt in Aleksei's arms. If only they could stay here forever…

After a while, he disentangled himself from their embrace and sat up. Leaning over her, he gently brushed some grains of sand from her cheek. "Come. We must go back now. Look, you are shivering." He ran a stroking hand over her goose-pimpled breasts, and she jerked involuntarily at his intimate touch. He leaned down farther and kissed her nipple. Kate, her insides dissolving, looked up at him pleadingly.

"I think you need more loving, Mrs. Aleksanou," he decreed in a husky voice. He got up and pulled at her hand. Unsteadily she got to her feet, gathered her shoes and jewelry, and allowed him to lead up the rocky path to the villa and the warmth of their bed.

Chapter Nine

"Aleksei, what is it? What's happened?"

Kate had been woken by the insistent sound of the ringing of his cell phone. He'd answered it and had carried on a concerned-sounding conversation in Greek.

Aleksei turned to her and gathered her into his arms. He sounded worried as he explained, "That was my aunt. Eleni's in trouble. She went missing two days ago. She was found last night wandering on a remote road on the other side of the island, disoriented and high on drugs. She was also covered in bruises."

"Aleksei, how awful! Was she badly hurt?"

"She's okay, but in a highly agitated state. The police think she fell in with a bad crowd of kids who've been renting two holiday villas up at Pelaphonia. Apparently, they've been holding all-night raves."

"Oh. I'm so sorry. Your aunt must be worried sick."

"She is. Eleni is already very fragile, and this won't have

helped. I think we should fly back first thing tomorrow."

Kate nodded her agreement, surveying her husband's profile in their darkened bedroom, the only light coming from shards of early September sunlight that had found their way around the drawn blinds at the windows of the apartment. She wanted to help, to get to know Eleni better, but the girl was hard to reach and her family so very protective of her. She touched Aleksei's arm in support as he got out of bed. She watched his magnificent physique, tall, brown, and muscular, as he moved toward the blinds and opened them onto a view of the River Thames. Then he headed off to the en suite bathroom, and soon Kate could hear the sound of the shower.

Since their wedding, he'd been away working for a while, winding down his presence at his London and Athens offices. But when he'd been home, their nights had been feasts of raw, instinctive passion, and by day their relationship had assumed a pleasant, companionable rhythm, full of conversation and laughter. She stretched languidly; she realized she was content in a way she'd never known before.

Although, every now and then, she saw the shadows that would cloud his eyes. Those times when they came were when she still didn't know how to cross the gulf and truly connect with him.

Her musings were interrupted by Aleksei as he emerged from the bathroom, a towel wrapped around his waist, his broad, bronzed chest glistening with droplets of water. At that moment, her hand flew to her belly.

"Kate! What is it? Are you okay?" He strode over to her side of the bed.

"It's just the baby…ooh! Here—" She took his hand and

placed it on her bump. "I've been feeling little flutterings for a while."

He squatted down and moved his hand. "I can't feel him yet."

"*He?* He could be a she!"

"No, definitely if you are feeling kicking already, it must be because it is caused by the boy's big feet."

"Then he must take after you," she retorted.

He laughed and rose to his feet. "He will grow up to be the most successful soccer player in all of Greece. Seriously," he continued in a more efficient tone, "are you up to going into the office today and then finalizing the arrangements with your apartment?"

She heaved herself upright from where she'd been lying back against her pillows.

"I'll be okay. I've got to collect my stuff and drop off the keys with the real estate agent. He's already got interest from prospective buyers."

"You'll have no trouble selling it. Affordable property is so sought after in London at the moment," he reassured her, then continued, "I have a day pretty well full of meetings, so I suggest you let Tino drive you in the limo to your apartment. Take Susan with you to help you with the boxes, then have Tino return you home to dress for dinner." His face darkened. "Then you and I will go on to meet Charlotte, though I would much rather that we have a quiet evening to ourselves."

"All right. I haven't got much to pick up." She smiled mischievously. "I'm looking forward to meeting your step-mother. I've heard so much about her!"

He didn't return her humor. "You haven't heard the half

of it when it comes to that witch," he said grimly, picking out a clean shirt from his closet. "Now, would you like some tea?"

At lunchtime, Kate arrived at the premises of Aleksanou Associates, having spent the morning with her parents, who had traveled to London to meet up again their daughter and her new husband. Yesterday, she and Aleksei had had lunch with her mother and father. Mr. and Mrs. Burrows had thoroughly taken to their son-in-law and were thrilled at the prospect of becoming grandparents. Earlier today Kate and her mother had gone to Selfridges department store and spent a pleasurable hour choosing clothes for the baby. After that they'd met Kate's dad and excitedly discussed when her parents would travel to Naxea to visit once the baby arrived.

At Aleksei's office, Kate was shown up to the boardroom, where the rest of the staff were waiting to toast the marriage of their CEO and former colleague.

"I want to thank everyone here for their support, hard work, and kindness," Aleksei announced to the assembled throng. "It is going to be very hard to leave you, the dedicated team who have helped to make my business what it is. But"—he turned to Kate, who was standing by his side—"I have the best reason to go…" He took her hand and gave her a kiss, then placed an arm around her shoulders. "And you have an excellent new managing director in Anthony Montgomery, who will guide and lead you. But you haven't entirely gotten rid of me. I promise that I will force myself to tear myself away from my beautiful wife and our child to come and join you for a few days every month."

While everyone aahed and applauded, Aleksei's eyes met Kate's shining ones. In his own way, he did have genuine affection for her, she realized, whereas she now felt something more…

A t seven thirty p.m., Kate was helped out of their taxi by Aleksei in front of the newest and trendiest restaurant in town. She wore the Grecian dress he'd bought for her in Thira, and she applied her makeup carefully to enhance her glowing complexion. She'd also put her hair up, a few wispy tendrils escaping here and there.

But no amount of grooming could calm her nerves. Aleksei's lack of enthusiasm for his stepmother was getting to her. Was Charlotte really a witch? Judging by his glowering expression, lit by the gas-fired torches outside the restaurant, she might be. Kate linked arms with Aleksei and gave him a reassuring pat. "Let's go meet Charlotte…"

"I wonder if she brought her broomstick," he grumbled.

Charlotte was already seated at their table. She rose as the waiter escorted them over. She was a tiny woman, curiously voluptuous of bosom, yet birdlike overall. Dressed in a low-cut electric-blue gown shot with silver thread, she was tanned to a deep mahogany, and her thick dark brown hair was teased and tumbled around her unnaturally taut face, her feline green eyes fringed by thick false eyelashes, her mouth a slash of fuchsia pink. She held out a heavily beringed, clawlike hand tipped with matching fuchsia nails. Aleksei surprised Kate by taking the hand and kissing it with exaggerated charm.

"Charlotte, how lovely to see you!"

The older woman gave a glassy smile. "I was so sorry

to miss your wedding, darling," she apologized in slightly accented English. She turned to Kate. "But I so wanted to meet your new bride." She leaned in, and Kate kissed her on both cheeks, her nostrils assaulted by Charlotte's heavy, musky perfume.

They sat down, and Aleksei took charge of the conversation and ordering some wine and water for Kate. If he disliked his stepmother, it didn't show. His natural charisma flowed, and Kate watched, fascinated, as Charlotte simpered and preened under the spotlight of his attention.

But as their meal was served and wine consumed, Charlotte's inner snake began to hiss.

"So, *chérie*," she said, turning to Kate, tapping her arm with a pink talon, "you were Aleksei's secretary, I hear."

"His personal assistant," Kate corrected.

Charlotte's green eyes glinted. "Aleksei always did go for working girls."

"Charlotte!" Aleksei warned.

His stepmother ignored him and prattled on, "Talking of which, I bumped into your predecessor in Paris, Phoenix Jones. She was hoping to land a contract with one of the top cosmetics brands there. But then you already know that, don't you, darling?" Charlotte shot Aleksei a beady look.

Kate stilled at the mention of Phoenix's name, then turned to Aleksei, whose jaw had gone rigid. "Yes, I also happened to run into her in London a couple of weeks ago," he explained stiffly.

Kate felt her spine shudder. He was silently furious, she could tell. But so was she—why hadn't he mentioned it? Charlotte, however, seemed very pleased with herself. Kate decided not to pick up on Phoenix in front of her. But

Charlotte had already moved on to other things.

"You're getting quite big already, aren't you, *chérie*? I hope you're not eating for two."

Kate forced herself to smile. "No chance of that. Maybe the baby's going to be a boy and take after Aleksei!"

"I think you'll find it quite challenging to lose all that baby weight after the birth. I can give you the name of a wonderful plastic surgeon in Paris who gives excellent tummy tucks. You can stay with me afterward while you recover."

"That's very kind of you, Charlotte," Kate replied through gritted teeth.

The rest of the meal passed in a whirl for Kate, as feelings of insecurity ran rampant through her. She sat quietly and let Aleksei bear the brunt of Charlotte's venomous sallies. Her insides were churned up with anxiety. Had he seen Phoenix again on the off chance, or was he still *seeing* her?

At ten, Aleksei signaled the waiter for the check.

"Oh, darling," Charlotte complained, "why are you leaving so soon?" She turned to Kate. "I suppose that, being so large already, you need lots of rest."

Kate took a deep breath and caught sight of Aleksei as he threw his napkin down on the table.

"Charlotte, that's enough!" He turned to Kate, placing one protective hand around hers and his other on her bump. "Unlike you, who only ever viewed childbearing as an inconvenience to be endured in order to keep my father paying for your excessive lifestyle, my wife is enjoying her pregnancy. She and this baby are beautiful and precious."

Kate gulped as a wave of emotion washed over her. Charlotte's jaw dropped.

Aleksei continued, "I think we've said all that there is to

say. We have to leave now, as we are catching an early flight to Naxea tomorrow. We have to return home to attend to a family crisis."

"A crisis?" A glazed expression passed over Charlotte's face. "Is that wretched girl causing trouble again? One of her little attention-seeking escapades?"

"If by 'that wretched girl' you mean your daughter Eleni, then, yes," Aleksei grated. "But it's not attention seeking, it's a cry for help, Charlotte. She needs some parental love and guidance."

"Well, darling, you're very good at that. Telling other people what to do." Charlotte waved a liver-spotted brown hand, and the heavy gold and diamond bracelet on her wrist sparkled. "Unfortunately, I've got so much on at the moment, so I can't really spare the time to run after her. Did I tell you that I'm spending next week on Capri at Anna di Marco's villa? Such a nice time of year to go there, after all those awful tourists have gone home."

Aleksei settled the bill quickly, and he and Kate said their good-byes to his stepmother as she continued to bemoan their early departure. Outside the restaurant, a black cab was quickly summoned to dispatch them back to Chelsea and Aleksei's apartment.

"You're very quiet," he remarked, turning to her. "Recovering from our interview with the vampire?"

"She's quite a piece of work," she agreed.

"It's like drowning in a vat of poison," he said wearily.

"Thank you for standing up for me when she bitched about my size."

He gave her a bitter half smile. "You're welcome. I meant it."

There was another silence. She glanced at him under her lashes. His defense of her to Charlotte had touched her, but even so, the revelation about Phoenix was still eating at her. She had to ask him. "Did you see Phoenix when you were last in London?"

"Yes. I was on Bond Street. I ran into her when I was coming out of a restaurant after having lunch with Anthony Montgomery. I took her for a quick drink," he admitted.

"Oh." She bit her lip. "Why didn't you mention it?"

"I didn't think it was worth mentioning."

"It just seems weird, that's all. You talked about other people you'd met while you were here." She tried to keep herself from sounding petulant, especially since he was clearly already riled by his evening with Charlotte.

"It meant nothing, Kate," he responded flatly.

She shivered when he said that. It was a phrase that held bad, bad memories. She felt her world rocking precariously. She had to find out more.

"I hope we can share things with each other," she said, aware that her voice was shaky as her body flooded with emotion. "Be honest and open."

He turned his upper body toward her, his eyes burning with hurt. "Are you accusing me of being dishonest?"

"No! But I was hoping that we might be more open with one another now that we are married."

He turned away to look straight ahead, his strong profile silhouetted against the lights of the London streets as the taxi sped through them.

"Some things are not worth sharing. This was one of them." He paused. "I was hoping that, as you agreed to marry me, you trusted me."

She heard the edge in his voice and the sting in his remark. "I'm trying to," she protested.

He exhaled heavily. "But you don't."

"I can't when you have secrets that you keep from me!" she retorted, reacting to the criticism she thought she heard in his tone.

"And you don't keep secrets about yourself?" he said coldly.

Her throat swelled as tears pricked at her eyes. She knew he was right. But she couldn't reveal the truth about herself, not if that meant she might lose him. "That was unfair. I don't mean to," she mumbled thickly, "and I don't mean to pry, either. But it's just that we don't really talk about some things. It feels like you're keeping stuff from me sometimes."

"You are making a fuss about nothing. Your mind is working overtime."

His curt dismissal hurt and frustrated her. And she felt like he was tying her in knots. He wasn't hearing the words she was trying to say. She hung her head as she made an effort to form a calm reply, but he beat her to it.

"Kate, when you push me like this, I am disappointed. I am bored and tired of being pursued by women who have agendas. I thought you were different. Don't do this."

She felt as if she had driven down a one-way street and smack into a brick wall. One that stayed intact after the impact. "I don't have an agenda!"

"Look," he said in a slightly more conciliatory tone, "I understand that this is a challenging time for you, with lots of change. You're expecting a baby, you're adjusting to being married and living in another country, while I am away a lot on business..."

She lifted her chin, her eyes blazing. "Please don't patronize me, Aleksei!"

"I'm just trying to show some understanding when you're upset—"

"And why am I upset? Not because I'm married, pregnant, or anything else. But because you've avoided answering my question—why didn't you tell me about meeting Phoenix?"

"That's enough! There is nothing to tell about Phoenix. Now, will you kindly leave the subject alone?"

Her fists clenched into tight balls. "So I'll just have to take your word for that then, like a good little wife, will I?" she replied tightly.

Chapter Ten

"Katie—look!" Lydia squealed as the picture sprang to life on the monitor. "It's a real baby!"

"Of course it's a real baby," Kate replied, laughing, and saw how her child danced on the screen.

She was now twenty-two weeks pregnant and having her next scan to check the baby's development. The obstetrician—once again flown in especially from Athens—assured her that everything was coming along just fine.

And once again Aleksei wasn't here. Since their London trip and the argument about Phoenix, he had withdrawn from her almost completely. Most of the time, he had been away, preoccupied by business all over Europe—Paris, Rome, Athens, London. He had returned briefly for a few days during the last three weeks. She had to admit that, for the first fortnight, she had been too bruised, angry, and resentful to do anything about breaking down the barrier of near silence that had suddenly grown up between them.

There was a steely look in Aleksei's eyes and a set to his jaw that warned her he was still seething, too.

But in the last week or so, she'd simmered down and had begun to regret the separation between them: the nights were the worst, and she was withering without his touch. She had to admit, she held Aleksei in her heart now.

She tried to focus on facts rather than feelings to halt the tide of emotion that threatened to engulf her. The issue of Phoenix was unresolved; she wanted to believe him that the model wasn't a threat, but she needed to discuss it more fully. However, she wasn't going to apologize to get the conversation started, and Aleksei was probably too proud and stubborn to do so, either. So how were they going to going to call a truce and begin communicating again?

After they left the hospital, she suggested to Lydia that they go to a café and have lunch before Lydia went on to the bar where she was working the evening shift. It might help, Kate decided, if she confided in her friend, if only to stop her head whirling with emotion and try to straighten out her feelings.

Lydia's counsel was surprisingly sensible and unsurprisingly frank.

"You need to talk to Aleksei, Katie."

"I know. But, Lyd, it's not as easy as all that. He won't engage with me."

"Well, it's clear that you need to pick your moment. But you're also doing the dance of denial."

"What do you mean?" Kate asked, feeling a little prickly at her friend's candid and accurate observation.

"Let's just say that I get the feeling that you don't want to engage with him, either. What is it that you're afraid of?"

"That he won't talk to me…that I'm going to have to say sorry when I don't feel I was in the wrong." She toyed with the straw in her drink as more feelings rushed to the surface. "Oh, Lyd, I can't help wondering if he thinks he's made a mistake in marrying me because I've asked for too much from him emotionally, or if he's still seeing Phoenix Jones."

Lydia lifted up her sunglasses to peer at her friend. "I spy with my little eye a friend who has fallen in love. Do you really think he's still involved with Phoenix?"

Kate frowned and shifted in her seat. She ignored Lydia's comment about having fallen in love. "I have no idea," she admitted. "And that's the point, isn't it? I have no idea what he does when he's not here, because he doesn't really tell me."

"He's probably working night and day," Lydia observed. "Isn't that what he did when you were his assistant?"

"Well…yes. Punctuated with gazillions of affairs with beautiful women."

"But he wasn't sleeping with you then, was he? He wasn't going to be a father!" Lydia said brightly.

"No, but—"

"Katie, you're here, by his side, as his wife, in his home. That counts for a lot with him. You've already told me you think he feels affection for you. Isn't it possible that his outlook has changed, that you and the baby are all that he needs now? From what I can see, I'd agree that he actually cares about you quite a lot, but I think he's hurting after what was said in the taxi. And his reaction is to stamp on anything that comes along to hurt him some more."

"Well, I wasn't trying to hurt him. I just wanted to speak honestly with him. I'd say it's that he doesn't want to care."

"Maybe. But whichever it is, if you want to get a dialogue going, you have to help him over it. After all, he's a man!"

Kate had to smile at Lydia's simple optimism, but she also had to admit that her friend's outlook had a logic to it. Perhaps it was worth a try.

"I'm afraid I haven't got much experience of men. Remember that I lived in an emotional deep freeze for seven years."

Lydia gave her a rueful smile and squeezed her arm. "I know. But you need to believe in yourself. Believe me, Aleksei's no callow adolescent boy like Oliver Temperley-Smythe. That was then and this is now. Like I say, Aleksei's a man, a real man, and you need to work with that."

"So, Auntie Lydia, tell me what I should do."

"You need to get the ball rolling. And remind him that he wants you, Katherine. Remind him what he's missing."

Aleksei was due to return tonight from his latest trip to Paris. Kate had spent the day in preparation for his homecoming, trepidation having given way to excitement. She'd made Hestia understand with her newly acquired smattering of Greek that she would want a special dinner served for him, and she'd also made appointments with a hairdresser and beautician and spent a pleasurable few hours in the boutiques of Thira looking for something to wear that didn't make her look entirely like beach ball on legs. A renewed glow of determination had enthused her as she hoped they would find a find a patch of ground where both of them could allow themselves to drop the defenses they'd erected and start connecting.

She also felt pleased that his favorite painting of the little temple by day had arrived yesterday from London. He'd instructed its dispatch, and she had gone to special trouble to have Dimitri hang it on an adjoining wall in the atrium, so that it complemented its already-resident partner at sundown.

By the early evening, she was examining her appearance in the mirror. Her dress was simple: maxi length with filmy sleeves, in a floaty fabric with a Moroccan-style print that mixed multiple shades of blue. She also put on the bracelet that Aleksei had given her after their first time of lovemaking. He had given her a matching necklace and earrings since. She'd let her hair fall free over her shoulders.

Downstairs, the fire was lit in the open-sided grate in the living area, offering some welcome warmth on a slightly chilly October evening, and the table in the dining area was laid for an intimate dinner for two, with candles and flowers, while Hestia bustled happily in the kitchen preparing a special menu of Aleksei's favorite foods.

She'd really enjoyed putting together this welcoming, seductive homecoming scene for her prodigal husband. She was looking forward to seeing him, even if they had difficult things to discuss.

She started, hear heart leaping, as she heard him arrive home, dropping his case in the hall and asking Dimitri to put his car away in the garage. She waited a few minutes until she could be sure that he was settled in the living area, enjoying a drink served by Hestia, before she went downstairs.

He was sprawled on a couch, a whiskey in his hand, as he pointed the TV remote control at the giant plasma screen on the wall and tuned in to the news. He turned and looked up at her as she stopped at the threshold. One of his eyebrows raised in appreciation, and he put his glass down on the low table in front of him, then leaned back.

"Mrs. Aleksanou," he drawled. "Are you going somewhere special?"

"Actually, yes," she replied, her voice light and teasing, and made her way across the marble floor to sit down beside him.

"And where would that be?" he asked, looking at her with hungry eyes.

"To have dinner with you. Hestia has prepared your favorite foods and will be serving us shortly. You look exhausted. I know you've had an extremely demanding trip and you deserve some home comforts...some pampering..."

He observed her again, a smile playing around his lips. "So you have missed me, *pethi mou*?" he said huskily.

"I've missed you very much."

He paused for a second, then raised his hand to stroke her hair. "You look stunning," he said, his gaze lingering on her face, "and I have missed you, too..."

He breathed an inward sigh of relief. These last few weeks had been very difficult. Racing around Europe, trying to secure deals on new developments and also making sure the installation of his new managing directors in London and Athens was going smoothly had been stressful. And the fact that his wife had been hardly speaking to him hadn't helped. Admittedly, he had been very annoyed by that flare-up in London and the suggestion that his fidelity couldn't be trusted. And somehow, since then, he hadn't been able to see a way back to harmony between them.

However, as the days had passed and his anger had subsided, he'd become more and more fed up with himself as he'd realized that, perhaps, he had been harsh in lumping Kate in with other women he'd known. He so regretted saying that stuff about women and agendas. Old habits died hard, and he'd resolved that he needed to lose the attitude. He'd missed her, longed for her, wished that he could lose himself in her beautiful swelling body. If truth be told, he enjoyed coming home to her, sharing the everyday things of their life. He needed to do more of it.

He rose from the couch and took her hand. "Let's go and eat," he said. When she stood up, he watched as her dress fell like a waterfall of blue hues around her. Her pale, burgeoning breasts almost spilled from its low neckline, too.

Silently he led her to the candlelit dining table and went to the ice buckets where wine and water were chilling and poured her and himself drinks.

"What have you been up to while I've been away?" he asked casually.

"I had my scan. The baby's doing fine," she replied happily.

A smile curved his lips as he handed her a crystal tumbler of mineral water. "I'm sorry I wasn't there. So Dr. Leandros is pleased with your progress?"

"Oh, yes. And"—she took a deep breath—"he told me the baby's sex."

His gaze intensified as he felt a curl of anticipation in his stomach. "So, do I have a son or a daughter?"

"A son."

"A boy. I was right about his big feet." His heart leaped. He couldn't keep the sheer pleasure from his expression.

"Yes, you were."

He took his glass and made contact with hers with a clink, wanting to show her his pride and appreciation. "To our son."

"And to us," she offered in return.

His eyes slipped lazily over her. "To us."

When dinner was finished, he leaned back in his chair and surveyed her as she quietly busied herself stacking up their used china and cutlery, the globes of her breasts quivering with her movements. He swirled around his brandy in a globe glass and watched her, yearning to push the gauzy material away and suckle what he knew to be her dark nipples. He felt his arousal springing to life, hard and insistent.

"If you chose your dress to tempt me, then you succeeded."

The atmosphere felt charged and heavy. Kate blushed as she finished her clearing away and discreetly tugged at her décolletage.

His eyes followed the movement, and his groin ached. But he was an expert when it came to women. The dress, the meal, it was all devised to charm him, wasn't it? He mentally shook his head. Hadn't he promised to himself that he wouldn't be cynical anymore, not now that he was married to a woman who was as guileless as they came?

Clearly, she'd gone to a lot of effort in order to clear the air between them, and he appreciated that. But his finely tuned instincts told him that something was still bothering her. He shook off his languid feelings of desire and decided to ask a straight question. There would be plenty of time for making love later.

"And I get the feeling that you are trying to tempt me because you need to talk to me, *agape mou*. Am I right?"

She stopped what she was doing to come back to sit down beside him, her aquamarine eyes pensive now. "I wanted to show you that I care, and that I care how you feel. But yes, I would like to talk." She hesitated, then the words tumbled out. "Are you regretting marrying me?"

What she said was unexpected, and it punched him squarely in the chest. He put his hands together in a contemplative steeple, then dropped his head slightly and closed his eyes. How had she come to *that* conclusion? He lifted his chin and opened his eyes again, then took both her hands in his. "Kate, how can you ask that when you have just made me the happiest man in the world?"

Now it was her turn to look surprised. "I have?"

"Of course. I am going to have a son. Do you know how much I have longed for this?"

He searched her face, and his thumbs caressed her palms as she gave a sad little smile.

"I do," she conceded. "You're pleased about the baby." Her eyes skittered away from his, and he had to incline his head to regain eye contact. He sighed to himself and reached with one hand to tilt her chin so that she looked at him again. "So, *hriso mou*, you think I am regretting making you my wife?"

He watched as her shoulders slumped and her eyes slipped downward. "I've been feeling bad after our disagreement in London." Her voice cracked slightly. "We've hardly spoken since. It just felt when I tried to get us to talk more, and be more open, you were angry and shut down on me. I began to wonder if you'd had second thoughts."

A finger of guilt jabbed at him. He'd been really annoyed by the way she'd prodded him about Phoenix. He'd tried to brush her off by telling himself he was busy with work, that she was suffering from pregnancy hormones and finding it difficult to get used to life as a married woman in a different country. She'd said he was patronizing. Perhaps he was. He took a deep breath.

"I was angry, but as time has gone on, more with myself than you. I shouldn't have dismissed your concerns like I did." He smiled ruefully. "You're going to have to be patient with me, Kate. Marriage and fatherhood is an adjustment for me, too. I've not been used to sharing my life and being with a woman who doesn't want me for my wealth, or just to get her face in the media."

He felt gratified when she replied softly, "You know I don't want you for your high profile or your money. I was just feeling locked out…and when I discovered that you'd seen Phoenix and not told me about it, I wondered if you were hiding things from me."

Suddenly, telling her what had happened didn't seem so difficult. "Please believe me that the meeting with Phoenix was totally unplanned. I stepped out onto the street and there she was. And after all the trouble I'd had getting her to let go, I thought it best to take her for a quick drink."

"All the trouble?" she echoed.

He sighed. "Listen. You remember when I finished my relationship with Phoenix while you were still working for me?"

She nodded. "I arranged for her to receive the ruby and

diamond necklace."

He inclined his head in acknowledgment. "That's right. Well, unlike other girlfriends I'd had, Phoenix wouldn't let go. I called her from the office that evening, but she became hysterical. I decided it was best to meet her one more time to make her see sense. I didn't want any more trouble from her. So I arranged to see her the following Sunday—"

"The evening after the morning when you slept with me," Kate interjected.

His eyebrows shot up at her sharp memory. "Yes. With hindsight, the timing wasn't great. But it was a situation that needed to be dealt with, quickly."

"I see." She paused. For a moment, he thought she was going to get angry again. "And did you deal with it?"

"Yes. She ranted and threatened. But I think she re-alized how turned off I had become by her behavior, and eventually she seemed to accept it."

"*Seemed* to?"

"Yes, I didn't hear from her again. Until I bumped into her in London. Maybe I should have just walked away, but good manners dictated that I should take her for a quick drink just to let bygones be bygones."

He was relieved when he saw that she couldn't help smiling. "You're such a gentleman." She lowered her lids and looked up him from under her lashes. "But maybe that's what I like about you."

"Oh, I'm not sure it's the gentleman you bring out in me, Mrs. Aleksanou…" His hand moved to caress her cheek, then ran down her neck to her breast. He leaned in and kissed her softly.

She closed her eyes, and he let his lips and tongue

capture her mouth and felt her aroused body responding to his touch. *Christos!* He needed her so badly.

"Come," he said gently, wanting to have her be with him the only way he knew how. He stood up and took her hand.

She rose up and stroked his cheek with her hand. "Thank you for telling me about Phoenix," she said, her eyes shining.

She allowed him to propel her to his bedroom, where he eased her down on to the bed and knelt over her. He lifted the skirt of her dress and parted her legs. She held her breath as he eased her knickers down and threw them aside. For seconds she lay exposed as he looked at her, thinking that he had never seen her look more beautiful. Then he bent his head between her legs and began laving her with his tongue, intent on giving her the most intense orgasm that she had ever known…

The next morning, Kate awoke to find Aleksei next to her, propped up on one elbow and studying her. "Good morning, beautiful," he greeted her seductively. "Can we start again?"

She looked at him tentatively. "I guess so. But…we still need to talk."

For a moment, he studied her speculatively, then he conceded, "Okay, how about after breakfast?"

"You don't have to rush off somewhere to seal a deal?"

"No," he said, "today I have all the time in the world for you." Then he surprised her by kissing her in the most leisurely, luxurious way.

Chapter Eleven

After they breakfasted, Aleksei told Kate that he was taking her to a visit a place on the island that had a special meaning for him. She was surprised and pleased at this gesture of intimacy. Perhaps it would be quiet enough there for them to really relax and talk.

He drove them along the coastal road. Though the temperature inland was mild and pleasant during the day and the sun still shined, there was a strong and faintly chilly wind down here, known as the *Meltemia*, that whipped northward off the sea. Kate was glad she'd worn a woolen cardigan and banded a scarf around her hair.

They passed the large old stone house that stood back from the road where Aleksei's aunt Dafnia lived with Eleni. Kate knew that the girl had been a continuing source of great concern for everyone since she had been found distraught and wandering after getting caught up with the gang of ravers in the hills back in September. Aleksei hadn't said too much about Eleni's state or progress, and Kate had done her best not to pry, though Marina had been more forthcoming and had explained that Aleksei had arranged for his little sister to spend some time in rehab in Athens. She was there now.

"How is Eleni getting on at the clinic?" she ventured.

A furrow marred his brow beneath his sunglasses. "She is doing okay. She is having therapy right now and we will know more in a couple of weeks' time."

"It sounds as though she is getting the best care."

"She is," he confirmed grimly. "They are experienced in treating drug addiction."

"I'm sorry," she said quietly.

"It is just one of those things," he responded tonelessly and kept his eyes on the road ahead of him.

Almost immediately, they slowed, and Aleksei turned the car along a narrow side road that quickly led to a secluded tiny bay, where the water was a deep blue and sandstone cliffs rose up on either side, dotted with small pine trees and lavender, marjoram, thyme, and other bushes. It was serene and peaceful, sheltered as it was from the wind.

He got out of the car and went around to the passenger's side to help Kate out.

"This is Sophia's Bay. But there is somewhere else that I want you to see. Are you up to a short walk?" he asked.

"Yes, I think so," she confirmed. "I'm wearing flat sandals. As long as it's not too steep and rocky…?"

"No, there's a path. It's just over the other side of the hill."

As they walked along the stony incline, Kate pulled her woolly cardigan around her a little tighter. Despite the sunshine, the hilltop was more exposed, and the wind from the sea was again strong and quite penetrating. When they reached the very top, Aleksei stopped and she did, too. Beneath her, she could see another bay, this one wider than the last and more exposed, with steep cliffs and coastal caves. Surprisingly for the Aegean, the tide appeared to have gone right out, exposing an expanse of sand, pebbles, rocks, and shells, and a worn stone pavement that led to a tiny island on which was perched a small classical temple of white stone.

The sight was wild and arresting, and she recognized the view as the one she'd seen in the two canvases now hanging in the atrium of the Villa Aphrodite.

She looked to Aleksei, who was standing very still beside her, staring out to the temple, his expression muted. They stayed there without speaking for some minutes, only the sound of the sea and wind breaking into the silence. She broke into his reverie by touching his arm. He started as if waking from a dream.

"This is the place in those two pictures that hang at home, isn't it?"

"Yes." He paused, then continued heavily, "It is also the place where my mother, Isadora, lost her life. She painted those canvases."

She was truly startled by this sudden revelation. She shot a look at him and saw that his face was etched with pain now as he looked again out over the causeway. She instinctively raised a hand to touch his arm, but he didn't seem to notice.

"I wanted to bring you here so that you would know what happened. That my mother died here trying to save my twin brother."

Shock reeled through her as she tried to take in this

new and terrible detail. "You—you had a twin brother?" she repeated slowly as she tried to comprehend the full enormity of the awful truth that he was unfolding to her.

"Yes, Andreas. He drowned here when he was just four. As did my mother, trying to pull him from the sea. It will be the thirty-first anniversary of their passing next week."

She took a gulp of the ozone-filled air. She'd had no idea.

"Oh, Aleksei, I am so, so sorry." She rubbed her hand up and down his forearm in a gesture of sympathy and comfort. "Do—do you mind me asking what happened?"

"No, I would rather you heard from me than from someone else." He took in a deep breath, then let the grim story unfold as she listened. "My mother was a trained artist, and she often came here to paint. This view was something of an obsession with her; she saw a lot in it. It was assumed that Andreas slipped out of my aunt Dafnia's house and managed to wander down here looking for her. But unfortunately a storm was brewing, as is common at this time of year, and the tide came in suddenly. Quite quickly, Andreas became stranded on Aphrodite's Point."

"Aphrodite's Point?"

"The small island where the temple is. My mother guessed that Andreas might have come here to try and find her. As I mentioned, she spent a lot of time in this place," he added, a hint of desolation creeping into his voice.

She looked at his profile, which had a sadness to it now as he carried on staring out over the causeway.

"There's a strong undertow in the bay when the tide is in. Others have also perished here."

"It must have been very difficult or you and your father," she ventured.

"Yes. My father took himself off to Paris to drown his grief in wine and women. That's where he met Charlotte. She was an aspiring actress." His gaze was hooded and bitter now. "I didn't see much of him after that, or her. They lived mainly in France, on the proceeds of the property business that my grandfather started in the 1920s. It was Dafnia's husband who kept things going until I was old enough to take over the reins. In the meantime, I was packed off to a boarding school run by monks on the mainland, and Marina and Eleni, when they arrived, were sent down here to be looked after by nannies and supervised by Dafnia."

"It sounds as if Dafnia was the strength in all your lives," Kate commented.

"She was the linchpin," he agreed. "Whereas Charlotte just cheated on my father and bled him dry until he died of a massive heart attack five years ago."

She just nodded silently and reached for his hand to give it a reassuring squeeze, because she was processing all that she had just been told and the depth of the tragedy that had been young Aleksei's life.

Then he turned suddenly and broke the taut silence. "Let's go and get some lunch. I know a taverna just a little farther along the coast where the food is delicious."

Accustomed as she was to Aleksei's ability to switch his emotions on and off, Kate confirmed her agreement with a faint smile and slipped her arm through his. Together they walked back down to the car.

The traditional restaurant was set a little way back up into the hills on the side of a steep winding road, next to groves of gnarled olive trees and cypresses. When Aleksei pulled up the car outside, the taverna's owner, an old man with a very brown, deeply lined face, came running out to greet him with delight. After the two men had exchanged pleasantries in Greek, Aleksei and Kate were shown to a wooden table set on a veranda heavy with vines in full fruit. The owner's elderly wife also came hobbling out and clapped her hands with delight when she saw Kate's pregnant tummy.

Up here in the hills, the temperature was kinder, and Kate enjoyed the rays of sunshine that slipped through the wooden roof of the veranda and warmed her face and arms now that she had taken off her cardigan. The air was gloriously clear and fragrant.

The meal took a while to be prepared, but when it came and was served by the devoted couple, it was simple and utterly delicious: smoky *taramasalata* and aubergine dip with pita bread baked on the stone range within, accompanied by a large salad of feta cheese, cucumber, tomatoes, and black olives, followed by sweet and sticky slices of *baklava*. The view from where they sat was also magnificent—green and gold hillsides running down to the turquoise sea. Aleksei relaxed in the sunshine and balmy air and told Kate stories of how he and his friends had often come to spend boisterous evenings at this taverna when he was younger before recklessly speeding back into Thira to dance until dawn at one of the town's discotheques.

After they had finished eating, they sat replete while she sipped mint tea and he strong, dark coffee. Impulsively she reached up and plucked a large green grape from one of the bunches that hung from the veranda pillars.

"Those grapes make great ouzo," he commented, "very strong and very rough."

She laughed, and as she did so he caught hold of her hand and looked deep in her eyes. "It means a lot to me that you are here with me today."

Her face became more serious as she entwined her fingers with his. "And I am glad that I am. Thank you for sharing what you did this morning."

"It's quite a story, isn't it?" he said derisively. "But I want you to know how it was, for you to understand."

She nodded. "Were you ever close to your father?" she probed gently.

"While my mother was alive, Andreas and I were the apples of his eye. But once she was gone, for all intents and purposes, so was he. To be honest, I felt abandoned," he admitted, "and I became a very angry, difficult little boy. That's why I was sent to Saint Dalmatius's, where the monks were big on discipline."

"I think I would have been angry and difficult, too," she empathized.

His fingers tightened around hers as he remembered again, "It will be thirty-one years to the day next Tuesday that she and Andreas were lost."

Kate found her eyes filling with tears. She had an image in her head of Aleksei, so small and alone, realizing that his mama and his twin were gone. She could see the emotion burning in his gaze as he told her, "The worst part was when their bodies were washed up on the seashore. They came back in together on the same tide. Though I never saw it for myself, I overheard the grown-ups talking and for years afterward I had nightmares about it."

She swallowed hard as she felt him loosen his grip on her fingers, though he continued to look at her with searing intensity. At that moment, she was aware of the baby kicking, and her hand moved in a protective gesture to her belly. She turned her head slightly, her vision misted over now.

"Kate, can you also understand now why it is so important to me that you and I are there, united, for our baby?"

"Yes," she whispered, turning her gaze back to meet and hold his, gently rubbing her tummy and trying to calm the gyrating infant. "Yes, I do."

"Ours is not a conventional marriage, but I feel in my heart that it can be a good one if we put our child first and support one another. I know I am not the knight in shining armor that you might have hoped for as a husband. But I'll always treat you well and with respect, if you will stay by my side. I need you, and our son will want for nothing."

She wiped her eyes as her heart lurched. He had admitted that he needed her.

She ignored the cold fingers of doubt that began strumming insistently, almost instantly, down her spine, reminding her that though he might need her, patently love still wasn't on his agenda. Maybe…maybe if they worked at it, he'd drop his guard and change his mind.

"Are you all right?"

"Yes," she replied firmly.

Chapter Twelve

Kate emerged from the grand department store on the Rue de la Madeleine, with Tino, Aleksei's driver and bodyguard, bringing up the rear laden with parcels and expensive carriers, after an afternoon of early Christmas shopping.

When Aleksei had suggested that she accompany him on his latest business trip to Paris, she'd had jumped at the chance. Naxea in late November was very quiet, and she realized that she longed for a little dose of northern Europe at the start of the festive season. And besides the prospect of Christmas, there was the feast of St. Nickolaos on December 6, when it was traditional in Greece to attend church, celebrate with family and friends, and exchange small gifts; she wanted to do her best to participate because she knew it would mean so much to Aleksei.

She was feeling very well, her pregnancy continuing to progress healthily. Her baby bump was prominent now, though nicely neat and rounded. It was only occasionally that her back ached a little. Her doctor had agreed that traveling in the luxury of Aleksei's private jet and then staying in a suite at the best hotel in Paris wouldn't do her any harm.

Anyway, she was, she admitted to herself as she settled into the back of the limousine while Tino loaded the spoils of her shopping trip into the trunk, greedy for time with her husband. Since that day in October when he'd revealed the truth of his devastated childhood, she and Aleksei had reached a state of closeness that previously she wouldn't have believed possible. Aleksei had not talked about his mother and brother's deaths again, but he had let his guard down enough to show her some more of his mother's paintings and talk further about his childhood. Kate realized that, quite probably, he had had never shared this information with anyone outside his family before. Now she felt she understood his driven, demanding nature a little better. She ached for the lonely little boy that he must have been, who'd learned to keep his emotions firmly battened down for fear that he'd lose any more of the most precious people in his small world, and for the adult who needed to keep control of everything that surrounded him.

At the same time, it was clear that he had grown up in an unhappy family. He was determined that their son shouldn't receive the same treatment.

Kate realized that she was becoming more open herself. What she and Aleksei had now was good, better than anything she had ever known before. She accepted that possibly she would never hear him say that he loved her—because he couldn't take the risk. But she knew she had Aleksei at his best and felt contentment. She was learning to live for and enjoy each day, and maybe one of those days, love might follow.

She was brought back to reality by Tino drawing the limo to a halt outside the grand, brightly lit facade of the hotel on the Avenue-des-Champs-Élysées where they were staying. Knowing that the handsome young Greek would carry her parcels and bags up to the suite for her once he'd parked the vehicle, she climbed out and entered the foyer, heading for the bank of lifts that would take her up to their rooms. Glancing at her watch as she waited for the elevator to arrive, she realized that Aleksei would have been back here for good half an hour now, after a day of meetings. She wished that she had remembered to take her cell phone with her when she'd gone shopping so that she could have called to let him know that she was on her way back, but she'd left it on the bedside table. She hadn't thought of asking Tino to call him from the car, either. Expecting a baby was addling her brain.

The lift doors opened, and she walked along the softly carpeted hallway, picturing Aleksei right now, probably stretched out on one of the huge sofas in the grand sitting room of their luxurious suite, his tie discarded, his shirt unbuttoned, a destressing whiskey on the table in front of him while he called Dafnia on his own cell phone or watched TV. When she arrived, he would tease her about how long she'd been out shopping and how much money she'd spent. And she would tease him back by telling him that she'd hit the limit on his credit card and giving him tantalizing clues about what she'd bought him for St. Nickalos's Eve and Christmas.

When she reached the main door of the suite, she let herself into the foyer and called out his name. "Aleksei?"

There was no answer. Then she noticed the lights were on in the bedroom. Perhaps he was in the en suite bathroom and couldn't hear her.

As Kate entered the bedroom, the strong, musky scent of an expensive perfume hit her nostrils. A punch of fright hit her as she suddenly saw the partially clad woman who lay on the silk-covered king-sized bed in an artfully arranged pose, bathed in the soft bedside lamplight. Her long and gorgeous tanned limbs were spread invitingly, the lacy red scraps of underwear she wore barely covered her breasts and private parts, and her spike-heeled, pointy-toed red patent leather shoes were impossibly high and shiny. Her long, poker-straight ebony hair framed the haughty beauty of her high-cheekboned face, which had graced the front covers of a hundred international glossy magazines.

Phoenix Jones!

"This is an unpleasant surprise," the supermodel purred, an nasty smile playing around her full, glossed lips. "I was expecting Aleksei. He promised he wouldn't be late…this time."

Initially, Kate was stunned. What the — ? Then a wave of fury rose up inside her, and she walked quickly to the side of the bed, where she grabbed hold of the silk coverlet and pulled it as hard as she could, causing Phoenix to sprawl out of her previous come-hither pose and lose one of her shoes in the process.

"There's no need to be like that," Phoenix said archly, trying to regain her poise on the slippery silk bedspread. Then she smiled nastily again. "I guess Aleksei didn't tell you that he was otherwise engaged."

"Get out," Kate yelled, seeing nothing now but a red

mist before her eyes. "Get out, you tart!"

"You watch your mouth, bitch." Phoenix's previously husky poshness became distinctly South London high-rise as she kicked off her remaining shoe, clambered off the bed in a swift movement, and got hold of Kate by her hair.

"You fat cow," Phoenix shouted as she swung Kate around, nearly pulling her hair out by the roots. "He doesn't want you."

"Let go of me," Kate screamed, tears of pain pouring from her eyes.

"Look at the size of you, you heifer. You thought that getting up the duff with Aleksei's kid would trap him, didn't you? Well, it hasn't worked. He can't stand the sight of you."

Kate stopped trying to unhook herself from Phoenix's red-lacquered talons and demanded, "How do you know what he can stand?"

Phoenix jerked her head up so that Kate as forced to look at the ugly sneer that curled the other woman's lip. "Because he told me." Phoenix continued in a menacing voice, "All those times you thought he was away on business—well, he was with me. Rome, London, New York. In fact," she finished triumphantly, "we never split up."

"No," Kate yelled. "You're lying." She tried to wriggle herself out of Phoenix's clutches.

But Phoenix held on tight and gave a mirthless laugh. "No, babe, you've got that so wrong. While you've been getting fat on that Greek island, he's been with me—getting some *real* loving."

Kate felt the blood draining from her face and clammy fingers of shock grabbing her throat. Gathering what strength she had left, she made one last attempt to free herself and banged against the bed, which in turn rocked against one of the bedside tables, causing the lamp that stood on it to fall, along with her forgotten cell phone.

At the moment, Tino arrived through the open door and, dropping all the parcels he'd been carrying, rushed to disentangle Kate. Phoenix turned on him and tried to claw at his face, but the bodyguard was too fit and agile for her. Soon he had the supermodel under control and in an armlock. Deftly grabbing her impressive floor-length white fake fur coat and draping it over her near nakedness, Tino frog-marched her away, but not before Phoenix had turned, with Tino dragging her now, and thrown a last insult over her shoulder at Kate, making a noise like a mooing cow.

Kate sat down on the messed-up bed and buried her face in her hands. Her scalp stung from Phoenix's assault, and she felt shattered. How had Phoenix gotten in here? Frightening thoughts tumbled through her mind. Could Aleksei have really been having an affair with the woman all along? A cold hand of fear stroked her spine. It was perfectly possible, she already knew that. Her brain ached as she tried to reason if Phoenix's claims could be true. He'd denied it, and she'd wanted to believe him, but maybe Aleksei *had* turned to Phoenix during those times when he'd been away.

That thought made her feel terrified and sick, and suddenly she was seized by an irrational desire to flee—she could get to the UK from here by catching the Eurostar train…she could ask her parents to collect her from St Pancras station and take her back to their home… *Stop it.* She couldn't just run away. Aleksei would be beside himself if he returned and found her missing. He'd call the police, and it wouldn't take him long to work out where she'd gone.

For a while she just sat and stared into space. No, running away was not an option. She had to stay, battle it out with Aleksei, try once more to get the truth from him. She glanced at her watch: he would arrive back at any moment. She had to get herself together. She rushed into the bathroom and did her best to straighten her hair and makeup and smooth down her clothes while thinking through how she was going to handle it.

When she emerged, she found Tino in the bedroom, attempting to collect her scattered parcels and shopping bags. He looked at her, troubled.

Kate thought quickly. Mustering the smattering of Greek that she had learned from Marina, she tried to get him to understand that she didn't want him to tell Aleksei what had happened. It was important that she got face-to-face with her husband first. Tino received her efforts mutely. In desperation, she threw her arms out in a wide gesture that circled the room, then she exaggeratedly placed a finger to her pursed lips to indicate silence. Tino seemed to comprehend this and nodded his head solemnly in assent. "*Ne,*" he agreed.

The next minute, they could hear Aleksei's voice in the suite's lobby calling for Kate. He strode into the lounge, and Kate came out of the bedroom to greet him, trying her best to keep calm and dignified, when what she really wanted to do was to hurl herself into his arms and rant and weep. The shock of Phoenix's surprise appearance was setting in now.

"I'm sorry I was late," he said, loosening his tie. "I should have called you. But I got caught up in a rather drawn-out negotiation."

"It's okay. I was quite happy maxing out your credit

card," Kate quipped, trying to keep her voice from shaking. As if on cue, Tino emerged from the bedroom, laden with her numerous boxes and carriers. "It was a very successful shopping trip, as you can see," she added, feigning a satisfaction that she did not feel.

Aleksei smiled as he surveyed her purchases. "Looks like you've bought up most of Paris."

"Yes, I'm not safe to be let out on my own," she replied swiftly, inwardly sighing with relief when he raised his eyes heavenward and laughed.

He turned to Tino and spoke a few words to him in Greek. Then the bodyguard departed, and they were left on their own.

Aleksei came forward and bent to kiss her. She closed her eyes and enjoyed the feel of his lips on hers and his warm hands, one of which slid around her waist, the other cradling her bump. When he pulled his mouth from hers and started nuzzling her neck, she asked, "Aleksei—do you mind if we just stay in tonight? In fact, I'd really like an early night. I just collapsed when I got back from shopping."

He raised his head, smiled and nodded. "Yes, of course. This trip has probably been a little too much for you in your condition. You need to rest. I'll order room service…and I like the sound of an early night…"

"Great." She met his eyes, her heart beating rapidly. "Actually, there's something I need to talk to you about—"

"Are you worrying because you spent so much of my money today?" he said in an understanding kind of voice.

"Well, yes, partly. I did go a little mad."

He lifted her chin and planted a kiss on her lips. "*Agape mou*, it's fine. It doesn't hurt to have a spending spree once in a while."

"No. But there was something else what I wanted to tell you." She could hear her voice becoming croaky as visions of Phoenix lying like a siren clouded her memory.

"What is it? Are you feeling unwell? Is it the baby?"

"No, it's not the baby."

He kissed her on the nose. "That's okay, then. Now, why don't you go and have a soak in the bath first while I get some food organized, sweetheart? And then we can talk." With that, he let her go and quickly turned to make his way into the bedroom before she could stop him. She hurried behind him. "Aleksei—"

He stopped inside the doorway and surveyed the scene as he saw the tumbled bedspread, lamp, and phone. He raked a hand through his hair, then demanded suspiciously, "Is there something wrong? Has something happened?"

"That's what I wanted to tell you—"

"I can smell perfume. Very musky, exotic, seductive… It reminds me of…" He paused as he searched his memory. He turned around.

She took a deep breath. "Phoenix Jones. It reminds you of Phoenix Jones. Because she was here."

He reeled around, his eyes piercing on her now. "What do you mean, Phoenix was here? When was this?"

"Just before you got back—just after I got back. I—"

"What the hell happened? Is that why the room is messed up?" he asked incredulously.

She wrapped her arms around herself in an effort to calm down, sensing that anger was bubbling away inside him. "There was a tussle."

"A tussle? What is a tussle?" It was clear that Aleksei's

usually wonderful command of English had temporarily deserted him.

"A…a fight," she admitted with a sigh.

She wished that she hadn't said it when he responded, "You were involved in a fight? Are you hurt?"

"No. But she nearly pulled my hair out."

"Kate, you are not talking sense. Who pulled your hair?"

"Phoenix."

"Phoenix? *Phoenix?*" he repeated. "This is unbelievable. Why on earth would she come here?"

She shook her head, gritting her teeth at his apparent incomprehension of what she was trying to tell him. "I have absolutely no idea. I thought you might be able to tell me," she replied stiffly.

He held out his palms. "This is as unbelievable to me as it is to you. I have no idea why Phoenix should come here."

"That's not what she told me," she responded as her chin lifted challengingly.

"So what did she tell you?" he inquired sharply, his brown eyes molten.

She tried very hard to bite back the confrontational note that was bursting in her throat. "Phoenix was waiting for me when I got back. I don't know how she got in here. She was lying on the bed wearing very little. She implied that you and she had never stopped your affair…that you'd been seeing her all the time we've been married."

"That's ridiculous," he exploded. "I've explained to you what happened with her. I haven't seen or heard from her since that chance meeting in London. Are you sure it was her?"

She felt tears of frustration and annoyance spring at the

corners of her eyes. "Of course, I'm bloody sure it was her—she was pulling my hair out, for God's sake," she shouted.

"Okay, okay." He pulled her to him once again and wrapped his arms around her. "Shh, my darling, calm yourself. Let me just talk to Tino." He stepped away from her and reached for his phone, hitting a speed-dial number. Seconds later, he was talking to his bodyguard. Kate's minimal Greek allowed her to understand, from Aleksei's side of the exchange, that Tino was confirming what had occurred. Her heart missed a beat. Thank goodness Tino had spoken up, despite her telling him not to.

He finished the call and stared at his phone for a few seconds. Then he turned and faced her. "So," he said slowly, "Tino has corroborated what happened—how Phoenix was wearing only her underwear, that he pulled her off you…"

She hugged herself again as she recalled the catfight. "It was horrible, Aleksei. She said that you can't stand me and that while I've been, and I quote, 'getting fat on a Greek island,' you and she have been together."

He moved toward the messed-up bed and sat down heavily. He put his head in his hands for a few seconds, then rubbed his face and looked up at her. "Come and sit by me." He caught hold of her hand and pulled her down onto the bed. "Listen, *pethi mou*," he said in a firm, level tone, "I have *no* idea how Phoenix found out we were staying here, or how she got into the room. I will find out. If someone on the hotel staff has blabbed, then heads will roll. What I do know is that what Phoenix said is complete and utter fantasy. There is nothing between us. As I already told you, I ended my very short relationship with her back in London, when you were still working for me."

She looked up him and said in a small voice, "I want to believe you, but how can I when this has happened…?"

"Kate, for God's sake, don't let this strange incident drive a wedge between us now. I thought that at last we were getting along as husband and wife," he grated.

"We are," she whispered. "But how did she *know* we were here? How did she get into our suite?"

"I don't know," he said shrugging and looking at nothing in particular, his expression troubled. "I think I told you before that Phoenix has had a hard time letting go. But even I wouldn't have believed she'd go this far," he said, suddenly sounding exhausted.

"How did she know you were here?" she persisted.

He sighed heavily. "I really don't know. My guess is that she's gotten to someone in my organization and dragged information out of them."

She looked up at him, frowning. "But who?"

"That's what I need to find out." He paused. "Do you trust me?" he asked, stroking her hair.

She jerked her head so his hand fell away from her. "I'm not sure…when I put it all together…" Her voice cracked as emotions warred within her.

He gave a bitter laugh. "It doesn't look good, does it? Seems like I'm going to have to prove myself to you."

"How would you do that?" She knew she sounded skeptical.

"As I've already said, I will hunt down whoever helped her to find us and get in here…and I will also prove to you that my fidelity is not in question." He sounded determined now. "I know that we don't have a straightforward relation-ship, that I offered you a marriage of convenience and told you that I can never offer you love." He shook his head. "Perhaps a psychiatrist would have a field day with me. But I promised you that I would be a good husband, and I meant it. I fully intend to always be there for you and our children. Please believe me." His eyes burned with intensity. "I am a man of my word."

Kate was struck by the feeling and apparent sincerity with which he said this. She wished she could believe him—she wanted to believe him. But after all that had taken place, only a fool would take him at his word. She needed to stand up for herself and her baby, protect him if it turned out that Aleksei wasn't being straight with her. And if he was, and he would go the distance for her to show her he was committed, fight for their marriage, then she wanted to see that, *needed* to see it.

She looked him unflinchingly in the eye. "Okay, prove it," she said firmly. Then, from somewhere inside an ultimatum rose up from and vocalized itself. "And if you're not telling the truth, Aleksei, then our marriage is over."

He speared her with his gaze. Something between a scowl and a smile played in his expression. "I will," he said grimly. "I most certainly will."

Later, they lay in bed together, Aleksei spooned behind Kate, asleep. Wide-awake in the darkness, she turned the evening's events over and over in her mind. When he'd reached for her, she'd refused him. How could she sleep with him while the jury was still out over Phoenix? She needed to feel secure, to have the absolute truth. A shadow had crossed his face and he had stared at her for seconds, then rolled away.

"It's okay," he'd muttered. "I understand, and I respect your wishes. Not until I can prove it to you."

When they got home to Naxea, she would have to move into a guest bedroom again.

That Aleksei had said he was going to prove himself to her amazed her; she knew that wasn't his usual style at all. It seemed like he really did care and want their marriage to succeed. But then again, she just couldn't work out how Phoenix had come to be here in this room tonight, or dismiss the fact that the woman had been lurking in the shadows the whole time she and Aleksei had been involved. Perhaps he just wanted to put up a good defense, fight this to a conclusion, because that was what he always did.

But it also pleased and amazed Kate that she'd set out her boundaries with him. Something in the relationship, and inside her, had fundamentally shifted. She felt a growing sense of power. No longer was she the emotionally scarred girl who'd closed herself off from getting close to a man. She was a woman who was about to become a mother, and she was recovering her self-esteem.

Though that didn't stop her from feeling as if the future was spreading out in front of her like a huge chasm. She'd jumped without knowing if there was light at the bottom, by giving him an ultimatum. If it turned out that he hadn't been honest, their marriage would be over. She'd taken a huge, huge risk, because she was falling in love with him…

Chapter Thirteen

During the month that followed the trip to Paris, Kate resigned herself to the barrier that had reerected itself between her and Aleksei again. To most of the outside world, she was sure, they seemed like a happily married couple, hosting a delightful meal for family and friends on St. Nikalaos's Eve. But behind closed doors, the atmosphere was strained and tense. They slept in separate beds, and though Phoenix's name wasn't mentioned, her presence followed them everywhere. But Kate wasn't backing down until she had her proof.

In the second week of December, Aleksei embarked on a business trip that took him to New York, and then London and Athens on the return leg. She wasn't able to stop herself from feeling relief. Living with distrust was horrible and exhausting. Aleksei was pleasant but distant, and she was on tenterhooks as to how he was going to prove himself like he'd vowed. She needed to hear it so badly.

The week before Christmas, Lydia prepared to leave the island. Not only did she have to spend the holidays with her mother back in England, but her big romance with Georges had petered out.

As they stood at the departure gate of Naxea's tiny airport waiting for Lydia's flight to Athens to be called, Lydia gave Kate a big hug. "What a pair we are, eh?"

"Yes," Kate sighed. "Maybe I'll be joining you in London."

"No news about Phoenix and what she was doing in your hotel room in Paris?"

"No," Kate replied listlessly. "It's like we've become stuck in a big black hole."

"Hmm," Lydia mused. "He needs to come up with something soon." At that moment, her plane was announced. "Good-oh, it's on time. Hopefully, I won't miss my connecting flight from Athens to London." She hugged Kate, hanging on for dear life, until Kate banged her back to make her let go.

"Katie, you know I'll always be there for you and the baby?"

Kate nodded, her eyes filling with tears.

"Ooh, come here —" Lydia made to hug Kate again, but Kate pushed her away. "It's all right, I'll be fine. Go. *Go.*"

"Okay, okay. Don't forget to text or phone me the minute you go into labor."

"I won't."

Kate waved until Lydia dashed up to the security

checkpoint, bag flying, where a rather wary official checked her passport and boarding card. Then her friend disappeared into the departures lounge and she stood feeling incredibly alone.

She made her way back to the airport parking lot, deep in thought. When she got home, she would press Aleksei about Phoenix. She couldn't go on like this for much longer.

When she got into the car, she noticed that all the magazines Lydia had brought especially to read on her journey were lying on the passenger seat. Her dizzy pal had forgotten every single one.

Kate picked up the top magazine: *Cool!*, a British glossy with lots of celebrity photos, fawning interviews, and gossip that Lydia had faithfully subscribed to by mail during her time on Naxea. She absently flicked the pages.

At that moment, her eye lighted on a large photo with a bolded headline next to it: LONDON: 15 DECEMBER. THE GREEK TYCOON AND THE SUPERMODEL. Her heart somersaulted and she did a double take as she realized the picture showed Aleksei leaving a top Chelsea restaurant with Phoenix. She felt a stab of fear and then the descent of dull recognition as she read the caption:

It appears that top international supermodel Phoenix Jones is living up to the meaning of her name, as her affair with billionaire Aleksei Aleksanou rises up from the ashes in a blaze of rekindled passion. Britain's catwalk sweetheart and the gorgeous Greek were snapped by the paps leaving one of London's premier restaurants—where fellow diners reported that they spent the evening deep in intimate conver-

*sation — before heading back to Aleksanou's luxury
riverside pied-à-terre. Could it be Bye-Bye (wife and)
Baby and more of Me and Ms. Jones instead for the
fickle property tycoon?*

For a while, Kate stared at the article, barely breathing.
Then she took in a great gulp of air. So he was seeing Phoenix
after all. Anger and humiliation burned in her chest; *he'd lied.*
Enough was enough. Her blood boiled. Without wasting any
more time on thought, and with her resolve stiffening with
every taut second, she started the car and headed at high
speed for the Villa Aphrodite, only just making some of the
bends on the winding road.

Just before Lydia left, they'd discussed what she might
do if Aleksei was being unfaithful, and once the baby
arrived. But Kate had been unsure then that she could really
and actually take that course of action, and had spent the
last couple days turning it over in her mind. Now, everything
was laid before her in stark relief: she had no choice but
to tell Aleksei that, as soon as the baby was born and old
enough to travel, she would be returning to London, where
she would file for divorce. She would not, could not, tolerate
his unfaithfulness.

Ever since Paris and her ultimatum to him, the realization
had been growing that, as challenging as a break with Aleksei
would be, it was possible. Of course she'd considered going
it alone when she'd first been pregnant. But back then she'd
concluded she didn't have the strength or the resources, and
she'd felt she had to give their marriage a chance. Well, she
had. But, clearly, he hadn't.

She tried to breathe slowly and get a grip of her racing

mind by thinking back to when she'd shared the story of Paris with Lydia. Her friend had been her usual optimistic, encouraging self, even offering to set up home with her if Kate were to return to London.

"We could share the child care between us," Lydia had volunteered enthusiastically.

"I think I'd demand that Aleksei hire a nanny as part of the divorce agreement, Lyd."

"My, how you've changed," Lydia had replied. "It's great."

"Well, I'm older and wiser now."

"That bad, eh? Though…" Lydia had shot a worried glance at Kate. "It does seem like you and Aleksei went from bliss to zero in just days."

"I told you what happened in Paris. The Phoenix incident really shook me up, and I've nothing to disprove what she claimed except Aleksei's word. I've always known that he'll never love me, but I had hoped our mutual respect would count for a lot."

"That, and a lot of great sex," Lydia had put in mischievously.

"Not even that now," Kate had sighed ruefully, raising Lydia's eyebrows. Leaving Aleksei's bed had been a bittersweet experience. That was the sole place where she'd been convinced that, deep down, he'd shown her a passion that was raw and rare…

"But are you sure?" Lydia had pressed.

"I haven't made up my mind," Kate had confessed, and at that point she hadn't. Should she stay and risk a lifetime of tension and loneliness? How would that affect the baby? Or should she go and attempt to function as a single mother?

But now, with the naked truth laid out in the magazine in front of her, she knew the catalyst had come and the decision had been made for her. She turned the pages to look at the date on the front cover: last week. That would be right. There'd been plenty of time for him to have hooked up with Phoenix while he was away. How dared he.

When she got home, she made her way straight to his study, where she knew he'd be.

She took care to gather her senses and knock politely before entering. He looked up at her unfocusedly. Obviously he'd been deep in some work. But he soon tuned in to her strained expression and taut air of determination.

"What is it? Did Lydia not get her flight?"

"Lydia got away just fine. But she left this behind." She placed the magazine open at the relevant page in front of him and fixed him with a hard stare.

For a moment, he stared at it, his brow furrowed. She stood, her arms folded, and waited for his reaction.

He picked up the magazine and chucked it across his desk, then waved his hand in a gesture of dismissal.

"It is nothing. I am not having an affair with that woman. I don't know why you believe this trash."

She found herself riled by his lack of concern for what she might be feeling.

"So why were you with her, if it was nothing?" she persisted. "Having an intimate dinner with her? Taking her back to your place? Are you saying these things didn't happen?"

"They happened." His cool lack of denial infuriated her.

"So how in God's name can you deny that you're having an affair with her?"

He gestured to the leather sofa that sat to the side of his

desk, next to a large floor-to-ceiling window that looked out over the terrace to the sea beyond. She didn't budge.

"Please, will you sit?" he asked. "I need to explain to you what really happened. I think you will feel better after you hear what I have to say."

She doubted it, but, her spine and shoulders very straight, she walked over to the sofa and sat down. He joined her as she perched stiffly on the edge of the seat.

"I would relax if I were you," he opined sardonically. "I have a great deal to tell you and we'll be here for a while."

"I'm quite comfortable, thank you," she snapped in reply.

"Okay. The first thing that you need to know is that I now know how Phoenix got into our suite that night in Paris, when you and she had a catfight—"

"I did *not* fight her. She got hold of me."

"Perhaps pulling her off the bed and calling her a tart wasn't the wisest way to handle her."

"She said I looked like a fat cow."

"I know." A smile quirked around the corners of Aleksei's mouth, but Kate didn't return it. How could he find this funny?

"How did you find this out? How on earth did she know that we were staying in Paris? How did she get into our suite?"

"That's why I arranged to have dinner with her. I wanted to know how she got hold of such information."

Kate gave him a disbelieving look.

"There are some things in life that need to be handled. That woman has already done enough damage. I needed to deal with her directly but also make sure that there will be no repercussions for us."

"I think it's gone too far for that, Aleksei," she said frostily.

"We'll come to that in a while. But for now, hear me out."

She didn't reply and waited, her fingers agitatedly twisting the edge of her sweater.

"Phoenix tried repeatedly to call me after I ended things with her, but I always had Susan screen the calls. As I've told you a number of times, Phoenix had trouble accepting that our relationship was over. However, Susan is not always the sharpest tool in the box, and I think she may have disapproved of my previous reputation with women. Phoenix was able to wheedle out of her what my itinerary was for the next couple of months and concocted a plan to try and ensnare me. Only she hadn't bargained on you joining me at the very last moment on our Paris trip.

"It seems that Phoenix booked herself into the same hotel as us. She set about luring a starstruck young bellboy into letting her into our suite. I hate to think what form the luring took."

Kate chose not to call the image to her mind. All this sounded too fantastic for words. "All right," she persisted tautly. "So you took Phoenix to dinner, and she confessed. But why did you have to take her back to your flat?"

"To meet my lawyers and sign an affidavit that she would not trouble me or you again, nor would she attempt to get any publicity about my relationship with her, or indeed my relationship with you. I can give you a copy of it if you like. It's very fortuitous that she recently signed a contract with a major French cosmetics house to promote a new line of theirs, and that I happen to know the head of that company very well. We built and sold to him his dream holiday home on another island in the Kephelades. He would have no hesitation in pulling out of the deal if I were to ask him to, and Phoenix, who is very greedy, is really keen not to let that happen.

"Unfortunately, the tabloids got wind of our meeting. And, as for Susan, well, I decided that it was probably best to let her go."

Kate nodded and pondered it all for a moment. Why would he make all of this up? "I don't know..." she admitted reluctantly, the wind dropping from her sails a little. "Okay, it seems as if you have it all neatly sewn up." She paused. "I apologize for doubting you. But...Aleksei, if you think that all this makes everything okay, well, it doesn't." She paused again and took in a ragged breath, knowing that she'd reached a low, low point. "So much damage has been done and so much distance has forced itself between us. It's difficult to know or see how we can close the gap or build trust."

For a moment, he looked at her as if he was reading her, and he didn't say anything. Then he replied gently, "Kate, I *have* told you the truth. I promised I would prove myself to you. I know this has been hard for you, but believe me, it is over now. We will not be bothered by that woman anymore—"

"Aleksei, listen to me. It's your turn to hear *me* out. That incident in Paris made me start considering if we would be foolish to continue on with this charade of a marriage." She heard her voice break but plowed on. "Since that night I've wondered if there's any real trust or intimacy between us." She stopped and stared him in the eye, her chin raised in challenge. "Why did it have to take a magazine article to make you tell me how Phoenix got into our suite? If you really cared about me, or respected me, you would have called me while you were away to reassure me, then explained to me last night when you got back. In fact, I have no good reason to know that you would ever have told me!"

He shrugged. "I was planning to tell you. But I was so far away, and as for last night, I got home late and I didn't want to wake you. It didn't seem a good time."

"A good time for whom? You? It always has to be on your terms, doesn't it, Aleksei? And that is my point. There is no love, no trust between us because you won't for a moment let either just happen. It can only be when you say. But I'm afraid that doesn't work for me."

"Kate, you're hurt and angry. And you're not thinking straight. There is no way you can abandon our marriage now. In another six weeks, the baby will be here."

"I know that," she said through gritted teeth. She stopped herself. "If I give our marriage another chance, I need you to trust me and be open with me so that I can trust you."

He got up from the sofa and went to look out of the window. For a number of minutes, he didn't say anything. She watched his perfect profile warily. He had his back to her and was apparently staring out to sea, his shoulders set. Eventually, he turned to her and spoke. He looked pensive.

"I have noticed when we've been together these last few weeks that you have been even more withdrawn than usual and preoccupied. You've obviously been giving the prospect of leaving a lot of thought," he observed gently.

She put a supportive hand underneath her pregnant belly and placed the other on her bump, rubbing it absently, almost as if she thought she could make contact with their son. "I have been thinking about it. This Phoenix thing really made me doubt if we can make our relationship work. I'm only human, Aleksei, and I need reassurance. A lot has happened to change my life completely in a few short months. I was single for years before I slept with my boss, found out that I was pregnant with his baby, was forced to come and live on the other side of the continent and marry him even though he offered me little more than a financial and social arrangement—"

He averted his gaze, then took a step back around and stared out of the window again. "You make it sound as if I've shackled you in irons and treated you badly. What of the partnership we agreed to make, for the sake of our child?"

"I thought I could live with that," she said tonelessly. "But it's not really a partnership, is it? Partners need to talk, trust one another ..."

"I trust you enough to be my wife and a mother to our baby."

"But not enough to love me."

"I never, ever led you to expect anything beyond what I told you I could offer you," he said quietly.

She inwardly winced as she felt herself smash headlong into that familiar brick wall at the end of the cul-de-sac again. "No."

He rubbed the back of his neck. "You knew how I was before I married you. You saw how I lived my life. In fact, you helped me arrange to live it. You knew I was selfish and not beholden to any woman."

She briefly closed her eyes as she recalled how she would act as a human barrier between him and the long line of women who had queued up to worship at his feet.

"But, you know," he continued, "a lot has happened to change my life, too, in a few short months, and I have made adjustments. I have left my old life behind completely. No more women, only you. I have made changes, too," he insisted softly, "and I was hoping you would see that." He turned, walked around the sofa to come to stand in front of her. "I admit I have been selfish, but so have you. Because you live inside your head and never share what you really feel with anyone."

"I'm not selfish," she flared defensively, knowing she sounded like a small, very angry child.

He raised an eyebrow. "There are things that you haven't told me about your past."

She looked down as she unconsciously clenched her fists. She couldn't deny that she hadn't revealed everything and that her fear had made her very hypocritical. "I know," she replied dully. Her shoulders slumped as a tsunami of regret flooded over her; why, oh, why, hadn't she been more up front with him?

For seconds he stared at her, then he let out the air from his lungs in a long slow hiss. He sat down on the sofa beside her. "I can see that whatever it is, it troubles you greatly." He took her hand, and his thumb circled her palm. "Perhaps both of us haven't been as open as we should, and now is the time to begin talking. I can if you will. Can we draw a line in the sand here, and truly start over?" A lighter note entered his voice. "And, you know, Christmas is coming, a time for family and forgiveness. What do you say to us using a little of the festive spirit to get a better understanding of one another? Unless, of course, I am making you really unhappy. If that is the case, say so now. Know that I am saying this against my better judgment, but if you feel you cannot bear to be around me, you will have your divorce."

Kate peered at him warily from under her lashes. His last words had cut their way through her heart like a knife. Now that he was raising the prospect of divorce, it felt brutal.

In truth, they'd been intimate strangers until now, but what he said about Christmas and forgiveness had touched her. She thought of family Christmases past and how her parents' home had always been a haven of warmth for her and any visitors; she'd like something similar for herself and the baby in the future. Aleksei's idea about drawing a line, starting over, struck a chord. It was a chance, an opportunity to begin anew. She cared enough about him to take it.

That last realization had her searching for the right words to answer him. *She loved him.* She'd come to the brink, and she didn't want to make the leap after all; he'd thrown her a lifeline. She squeezed his hand.

"I don't want a divorce if I can help it," she said levelly. "I want us to try and make a go of it."

He pulled her forward, and his lips brushed her forehead. "I'm so glad, *pethi mou.* You will not regret it." He kissed her again.

Chapter Fourteen

On the twenty-third of December, there was a surprise delivery to the Villa Aphrodite of a real spruce Christmas tree and huge boxes of decorations, holly, and mistletoe, plus a hamper of seasonal foods and confectionery, courtesy of Fortnum and Mason, a top-notch department store in London.

Tears filled her eyes, and she watched, overwhelmed, as Hestia and Dimitri unwrapped a giant plum pudding and accompanying jar of brandy butter. She was, she had to admit, totally overjoyed by Aleksei's gesture of bringing a British Christmas to the Greek islands. She'd been feeling a little wistful, being so far from her home country, but now she had a taste of it here.

He was really trying to prove himself, she thought appreciatively. Things were good between them now, although they had not yet talked, nor had she returned to his bed yet; there were still some miles to go on their journey to closeness and true intimacy. In some respects, they were like shy teenagers, and Aleksei was wooing her. It felt nice.

Dimitri had planted the tree in a terra cotta tub appropriated from the terrace, and as the evocative scent of pine filled her nostrils, Kate made her way across the atrium to where the tree proudly stood and began riffling in one of the boxes. She pulled out an exquisite silver-and-glass globe and carefully hung it on one of the beckoning branches. An hour later, she had created an object of beauty, decorated in silver and gold baubles, small colored birds, snowy tinsel, and crystal icicles. She was just about to mount a stepladder to place a cute ruddy robin on a high branch and then the Christmas angel at the very top of the tree, when she felt an arm reach around her waist and the warmth of Aleksei's lips as they made contact with her neck. For a brief moment, she reveled in the strength of his body, his five o'clock shadow as his chin grazed the side of her face, the citrus smell of him.

"If you think that I am going to let you climb that ladder when you are as pregnant as you are, then you have another think coming," Aleksei warned her in rich, chocolate tones.

"I'm not that big," she retorted. "Anyway, you aren't going to stop me putting the angel at the top of the tree and making a Christmas wish."

"Then we must go up the ladder together."

She let him help her up the rungs as Dimitri steadied the ladder down below. He held her hips while she stretched up and fixed on the behaloed figure.

"What's your wish?" he whispered in her ear as they both made contact with the floor again.

"That the baby is born happy and healthy," she replied fervently.

"That is a good wish. I wish it, too." He kissed her neck again, and for a blissful moment they stood together.

"I shouldn't have told you what I wished, because it won't come true," she muttered and clammed up straight away when she realized what she had said.

"It will if I have anything to do with it," he replied, half under his breath. She felt her heart leap. She had a brief premonition in her mind of Christmases yet to come, of her small son playing under the tree, gleefully unwrapping his presents, while she and Aleksei looked on indulgently. She longed for that kind of happiness; maybe it was now within reach.

Her reverie was broken by Hestia coming from the kitchen, bearing a tray of hot chocolate and *melomacarona*—traditional Greek seasonal cookies. As she, Aleksei, Hestia, and Dimitri stood around the tree sipping their drinks and munching, the housekeeper and her son staring at the decorated tree in awe and pleasure, Aleksei remarked, "Tomorrow, Dimitri and I will go into the forest and get us a Yule log."

"A Yule log?" Kate repeated.

"Yes, it is a Greek custom to have a log burning in the grate for the twelve days of Christmas. I will light it just after midnight on Christmas morning. I believe that they used to do the same in England hundreds of years ago."

"Yes, I think you're right, they did," she agreed, surveying her husband with pleased surprise. "I never realized that you were such an ardent observer of tradition," she added, a touch mockingly. "Will you be killing a pig on the way as well to bring back for roasting for our Christmas lunch?"

He laughed. "No. We eat turkey in Greece these days,

just the same as you do in Britain. We will be having a large bird with all the trimmings."

And they did, the very next night, which was Christmas Eve, at a late dinner held at Dafnia's house. After a church mass and *kalandas*, Greek carols, Aleksei's family was gathered around the table, including Eleni, who had returned from her stay in rehab looking fresh and serene. Kate was enchanted by it all.

As she and Aleksei were preparing to leave, Dafnia came over to her, leaning on her cane, and hugged her. Kate thanked her profusely for the lovely evening. "Our pleasure," the older woman returned in her faultless English. "It is wonderful to have you as part of the family. You have made Aleksei very happy. Next year we will look forward to celebrating with my great-nephew." She laid a gentle hand on Kate's tummy.

Kate smiled warmly and placed her own hand over Dafnia's. She hoped so, so very much. "Thank you for making me feel so welcome."

During the drive home, Kate stared out at the dark landscape as it sped by. After some very clement and mild weather, it was starting to rain and getting windy. A storm was forecast for Boxing Day, the twenty-sixth. It would be the feast of St. Stephen here in Greece. She became aware that Aleksei was throwing glances her way as he steered the car along the winding road. Things were so much better between them, though they still needed to talk about a few things. She shivered. She would have to tell him about her first pregnancy. Without realizing it, her face knotted with anxiety as familiar feelings of humiliation and inadequacy flooded through her veins, and pain twisted in her gut.

"Penny for them," he probed. "Not having second thoughts, are you?" he added warily.

"No." She shook her head. "I'm having a lovely Christmas." She forced herself to sound upbeat.

"I'm glad. My family have really enjoyed having you be part of things. My aunt is so looking forward to spending next Christmas with her great-nephew."

Kate smiled through the darkness. "She told me. She a lovely, lovely lady."

"This has to be one of the happiest Christmases I've ever spent." He slowed the car and pulled over in a passing place by the side of the road. For a moment, both of them sat there and said nothing. Kate watched drops of rain flying at the windshield and noticed through the glare of the car headlights the small religious shrine that had been set up a few yards away, with its burned-down candle and dead flowers. She turned and looked at Aleksei, who was sat, his hands draped over the steering wheel. He turned in response to her gaze and looked at her, too. In the dim illumination caused by the throwback of the headlights, she thought she could see need etched on his face. Involuntarily and instinctively she reached out to touch his cheek and stroke it. His hand rose to catch hers, then he turned her palm to his lips and kissed it tenderly. Her stomach somersaulted as his lips caressed her skin, and she trailed her fingers down his face, her hand falling from his grasp to his chest.

As if she was being drawn by an invisible thread, she leaned forward and laid her mouth on his. She welcomed his invading tongue as it probed and tangled with hers, gently at first and then demandingly. She found herself melting into him, and his arms surrounded her, one of his hands rising to tangle in her hair. She could feel the heat of him, the weight of him as he pressed her back against her seat, his mouth crushing and greedy, and she welcomed it all. He grabbed her hand and moved it down over his taut stomach to his groin and placed it on his arousal.

"Touch me."

Kate did as she was bidden, and as she opened his pants and slid her hand under his boxers to place it on his hardness, it felt like she had touched a red-hot poker, so fierce was his erection.

"Oh, Aleksei. Oh my God," she moaned.

For seconds, he just stared at her, his chest rising and falling as he breathed hard. His mouth caught hers in a long, passionate kiss. Then he drew back from her, hissing, "*Christos!*" and pivoted around and started the car engine and skidded off.

They reached the Villa Aphrodite in record time. After screeching to a halt outside, he shot out of the car and raced around to open the passenger door. Propelled by some invisible force, she heaved herself out of the car and rushed into his arms. He pushed her up against the vehicle, the rain soaking them both as he sought her mouth again and plundered it with his tongue. She groaned, and her hands tore at his jacket.

"We need to get inside, *agape mou*, or I will take you here," he grated.

The atrium and living area of the villa were deserted. The tree sparkled next to Isadora's painting of Aphrodite's Point at sunset. They kept on going until they reached Aleksei's bedroom. He threw the door wide open. She walked past him and then turned to face him. They stood, just surveying each other, Kate's chest rising and falling with pent-up desire. Then he walked swiftly toward her and caught her mouth roughly with his, forcing her head back. She didn't resist as he moved her toward the bed, then pushed her gently down onto it. He stood back from her, and she watched, her heart in her throat, as he undid his shirt to reveal his muscled, bronzed chest covered with crisp dark hair.

He came down beside her on the bed, then without words rolled her firmly on to her side and pulled her up on to all fours, pushing her knitted wool shift dress up and pulling down her leggings and knickers. She was aware that she was exposed to him as he pushed her legs farther apart and unzipped his trousers. There were no preliminaries as he entered her with a firm thrust.

He held still, his hands on her hips, and then he began moving inside her, making her gasp as his solid flesh made repeated contact with her soft moistness, sending waves of intense pleasure coursing through her. His rhythm was insistent and increasing, and Kate couldn't help pushing back and arching against him, crying out as he filled her in an animal mating. Finally, their climaxes near, he snaked one supportive hand under her swollen belly while his other hand reached for her shoulder as he pulled himself urgently into her and gave in to his release. She heard his hoarse shout, felt the hot rush of his seed, and let herself come shuddering to meet him.

When it was over, her limbs buckled, but he held her firm and lowered her gently down on to the bed and onto her side. He collapsed next to her, and they lay curled together, their hands protectively on her tummy, as they fell into a satiated sleep.

Kate was woken from a delicious long slumber by the sound of china being placed on the small bedside table next to her. She opened her eyes to see Aleksei, dressed in boxer shorts and last night's shirt open to the waist, standing over her, having brought her customary morning cup of tea and a large bowl of yogurt and honey.

"Good morning," he said pleasantly as he made sure the breakfast tray was securely laid on the table.

"What time is it?" Kate asked sleepily, struggling to raise herself from the bed, aware that she was still wearing her woolen dress.

"About ten o'clock." Aleksei reached behind her and pulled up the large feather pillows so that she could support herself more comfortably and handed her a cup of tea, which she sipped gratefully.

She watched as his hand went to a small package also on the breakfast tray. He handed it to her.

"What's this?" she asked, surprised, relieving herself of her mug of tea and taking the exquisitely wrapped object.

"Just a little something to say happy Christmas," he replied, his eyes dancing. "Open it," he urged. He sat down on the edge of the bed while she gazed at her gift.

Uncertainly she unwrapped the parcel. There was a small purple velvet–covered jewelry box inside, which she opened to reveal a delicate ring of rose-colored gold, the band scattered with tiny pink sapphires and diamonds.

"It's beautiful," she whispered, a rush of emotion and confusion covering her.

"It's an eternity ring," he explained. "I had it commissioned just after our wedding."

"Thank you," she said simply, feeling choked up.

He stood up and started walking toward the door. "Just going to get my coffee and then I'll come back to join you," he threw over his shoulder. When he reached the door, he stopped, his hand resting on the knob, and turned to face her with a meaningful look. "There's another gift I want to unwrap—slowly."

He turned and left the room, leaving Kate giggling and looking at the eternity ring. She caught a glimpse of an inscription etched inside the band: *Forever*. Her throat swelled up with a mixture of happiness and sadness: it meant so much that he'd had that done, but would she ever hear him say, "I love you"?

G uests were due to arrive for a late lunch at two, then the exchange of gifts. Kate got up, went to her own room, and washed and dressed in loose gray pants and a pretty emerald-green silk caftan. After catching her hair in a simple ponytail and applying a little makeup, she donned diamond stud earrings. Then she reached for her phone and put in a quick call to Lydia to wish her friend a happy Christmas. She'd call her parents this evening, as she knew they were going out for lunch with her grandmother to a country pub for a meal with all the trimmings.

Just as she was about to depart downstairs, she remembered her eternity ring, still sitting in its box on the bedside table in Aleksei's room. She went along and retrieved it. For a moment, she looked at it as it lay in the palm of her hand: it was the kind of jewelry she preferred—handcrafted, delicate, pretty, and unostentatious. She put it on the third finger of her left hand, above her wedding band. By placing it there, would it act like some kind of spell that would bind her to Aleksei forever?

Then she hurried along to the kitchen, where Hestia was preparing the food, and, donning an apron, got stuck in to help her.

The buffet lunch was a great success. The guests, including Hestia and Dimitri, tucked in to delicious lamb, chicken, and pork on skewers, salads, and dips. Kate had had Hestia steam the pudding and heat the mince pies from the hamper and served small portions of them with cream, ice cream, and the brandy butter. The English specialties went down a treat.

Later, as the Yule log glowed in the open-sided grate in the living room, which was bedecked with holly and mistletoe, presents were opened with squeals of surprise and delight. Kate had wrapped all the gifts she bought for Aleksei in Paris: a cashmere sweater, a gold and diamond watch that had inner dials, including one to show the time elsewhere in the world, a solar-powered touch-screen tablet, and a new aftershave, the scent of which had tantalized her nostrils. After he'd opened each package, he caught her attention briefly, and she could see how he was touched by her thoughtfulness. He pulled her to him and kissed her briefly on the lips, then searched her face, an intense light in his eyes.

Kate glowed with pleasure, then busied herself opening the gifts sent to her by her parents. She unwrapped a leather jewelry box, a cute onesie, and some gorgeous luxury bath products for mums-to-be. She slipped away from the celebrations and called them to wish them a happy Christmas and thank them for their presents.

The party ended just before ten o'clock, leaving Kate and Aleksei alone in front of the fire. She started tidying up the discarded wrapping paper that lay scattered around. Aleksei came to stand in front of her and put a restraining hand on her arm.

"Leave that," he suggested. "We can deal with it tomorrow. Let's just relax tonight and enjoy our log."

"Okay." She made her way to the sofa, where her parents' presents lay on the seat cushion. She picked them up and carried them over to a side table.

"Your mother and father were generous," he remarked as she returned to sit beside him.

"Yes. They always gave me wonderful Christmases when I was a kid," she responded wistfully.

"Do you miss them?" he asked, looking concerned and rubbing her back.

"Yes. It was hard talking to them earlier this evening," she confessed, settling back into her seat and wriggling as she enjoyed his hands skimming up and down her slightly achy spine. "I think they really missed not having me around this year, too. Ah, well, I'll be making up for it next year when they have a grandson to spoil."

"Your parents seemed so lively and enthusiastic when we met them in London. Very, very happy about their forthcoming grandchild."

"Yes," she agreed, nodding. But then she saw his expression had changed to something more thoughtful and serious.

"So tell, me, *pethi mou*. If you had such a happy

childhood, why do I have this constant feeling that you hide an unhappy secret?"

She stilled. "I don't know what you mean," she dismissed.

He stared at her, a deep frown now marring his otherwise handsome features. "On the contrary, I think you do know what I mean. Why are you so nervous?" he said, taking her fidgeting hands in his own.

"I think you're imagining things," she replied stiffly, praying that he would drop it.

"I don't think I am," he persisted. He caught hold of her as she tried to rise up from the sofa. "Kate, you're flustered and upset. I know you well enough to realize that you are not being straight with me. Tell me, what is it that troubles you?"

She sat on the edge of the seat, temporarily frozen. Nothing got past him. She let out a heavy sigh. What was the use of hiding what had happened? She had resolved to be more open, after all.

"Okay." She summoned all her courage and pushed the words out. "When I was eighteen and just started at Camford University, I fell in love with another student. He told me he loved me, too, but then I found out that he had only been sleeping with me to win a bet. He deliberately pursued me, reeled me in, and seduced me because I was a virgin— " She broke off because her throat was threatening to close up.

She hadn't been watching Aleksei when she told him this, but she glanced at him now and realized that he was very still. She tried to pull her hands away out of his and made to get up, but he held her fast in his grip. "It was all very sad and sordid," she said brokenly, half off her seat, half on, "but I was devastated… He told me the truth in front of a crowd of other students. He humiliated me." She broke down into racking sobs.

He pulled her back to him and wrapped his arms around her. "Hush, it's okay," he crooned tenderly. She burrowed into the warmth of him, gulping as the dry sobs started hitting the back of her throat. The sense of loneliness, the emptiness, the helplessness that had never really gone away loomed up and threatened to swallow her.

His voice cut through her isolation. "You said that the boy who slept with you for a bet…he chose you because you were a virgin?"

She made an effort to stop the flow of her tears. She sat up and rubbed her wet cheeks with the back of her hand. "His name was Oliver," she explained tonelessly, almost reciting the facts. "He came from a very good family—you know, breeding and money. We hooked up in the first week of term, and I thought it was love. I gave him my virginity." She stopped as she started hiccuping again. "But I…I found out that he had pursued me for a bet. He was a member of a…gentleman's club—like a fraternity in American colleges—called the Bucks. They were second-year male students going around targeting stupid, naive first-year girls. Whoever bagged himself a virgin won…"

"I hope you're not calling yourself stupid and naive, Kate," Aleksei interjected.

"But I was," she cried, tears springing anew in her already-reddened eyes. "I was fresh, willing meat. Apparently, other girls in my year saw them coming and didn't fall for it."

"Sweetheart, you were young. You…were innocent. You mustn't blame yourself. The Bucks, or whatever they called themselves, were wrong. Treating women like dirt."

He leaned his lips against her temple and kissed her. "If I ever met this Oliver, I'd take him apart, limb from limb."

She couldn't help smiling. "He's a successful internet entrepreneur now. I sometimes see his smiling face in the media, above articles about how he's made millions and he's only twenty-six."

He shook his head. "So that's why you were so buttoned-up and reserved when you were working for me. I couldn't understand why a woman as beautiful as you didn't have a boyfriend."

"Yes," she admitted, hanging her head. "I just shut down afterward. Like I said, it was totally humiliating. Everybody was laughing behind my back, so I left my university course, and it took a while to get myself back on track. I haven't dated or had a relationship since. I just couldn't bring myself to trust a man." She paused and said shyly, "I was amazed when you said that you wanted me."

She waited for him to reply. He pulled her back into his arms. She found herself falling into their welcome willingly and buried her face in his shoulder.

He stroked her hair. She lifted her head slightly and glanced up at him. He was staring straight in front of him, his hand moving almost absently.

"I'm sorry I didn't tell you sooner," she said, her voice muffled into his sweater.

"I wish you had."

"I thought you would judge me."

"I don't judge you at all," he levelly. "Sex is a dangerous, unpredictable commodity. I know that." He gave a self-deriding half smile.

She heard the bitterness in his voice and, lifting her head

fully this time, sat up. "What do you mean?"

He exhaled heavily and searched her face with his eyes. "There's also something in my past that I ought to have told you about before now. I was married."

She was startled to the core by this admission. "*Married? When?*"

"About ten years ago. Her name was Aella. Whirlwind by name, whirlwind by nature. She was a local girl, the daughter of a wealthy hotelier. I'd known her all my life and had been in love with her for half of it."

"Aella," Kate repeated. "What happened to her, Aleksei?"

"My father told me that she was shallow, ambitious, and flighty, but I couldn't see it. Throughout my adolescence, she filled my dreams. To me she was like a butterfly, beautiful, wild, and untamed, and I had to trap her."

"Trap her? But I thought you were a renowned playboy," Kate exclaimed, adding sheepishly, "There's no mention of your marriage in any internet profile I've seen."

"Ah, so you've been doing searches on me, have you," he replied, looking amused.

"Might have," she said, lifted her chin and smiling. "I needed to know who I was marrying."

"The marriage was actually very short," he admitted. "When we divorced, I paid her a large sum of money and had her sign a nondisclosure agreement, which she accepted willingly. I think she would have been quite unscrupulous about going to the press and selling her story."

"Do you mind me asking why you got divorced?"

"Aella got pregnant on our honeymoon and got rid of the baby without telling me. She didn't want to ruin her figure," he said matter-of-factly.

"Oh, Aleksei, how horrible," she breathed, stunned by his revelation.

He didn't answer, but continued, "After that, I decided that being a playboy was safer." He gave a grimace. "Like you, I put my heart on ice."

"What happened to Aella?" she asked after a while.

"She went to Athens, snared one rich Greek man, married and divorced him, then another, and last we heard, she'd moved to Naples and on to a member of the Italian mafia, who lured her into porn."

"Nice," Kate remarked, noticing his heavy expression. When coupled with the loss of his mother and the wounds inflicted by Charlotte, it was little wonder he had become so ruthless in his relationships with the opposite sex. "I'm kind of beginning to understand why you felt you'd never marry for love."

He shot her a look. "For a long time, I preferred the numbness of variety," he confessed. "But I've also come to know that making love with one woman and getting to know every inch of her is the best aphrodisiac in the world."

Her cheeks glowed with shyness and surprise. "Do you really mean that?"

"Yes." He looked at her and smiled fully. "You have taught me that."

She smiled back, her heart swelling as she savored his praise.

He raised a hand and pushed an escaped lock of her hair from her cheek. "And I'd like to learn it once more. Shall we go to bed? It's been a busy day."

Later, as they lay together, she listened to the steady sound of his breathing as he slept. She, however, was wide-awake, her head still buzzing with the emotion of this evening's revelations. She felt such relief at having told Aleksei about what had happened to her at university. The degree of compassion and nonjudgmental acceptance he had showed her tonight had amazed her. She had observed and experienced him to be ruthless in his relations with the opposite sex. However, after what he had told her tonight, she now understood that he could be as vulnerable as anyone else.

But, she reflected, their conversation had reconfirmed the one thing that challenged her the most: that he never would have married for love. Did his previous experiences mean he really lacked an inner loving core now when it came to intimate relationships? Was he incapable of giving her the one thing that she craved from him? She snuggled in closer to her sleeping husband's back and felt him stir slightly. One thing was definite now, and it had been a slow dawning, not the proverbial bolt of lightning. She loved him, she really did.

Chapter Fifteen

On New Year's Eve, Aleksei landed at Naxea airport on the first flight in from Athens. He'd been dealing with some unexpected legal hitches in a building project for a luxury spa on another island. He'd planned to return in time for to attend the big New Year celebration that took place annually in Thira, including a fireworks display over its small harbor. But a winter storm was predicted to blow in from the south, and it wasn't certain that the party would be able to go ahead. He'd wondered if this plane might be delayed because of the weather. But he was glad he'd made it home. Tomorrow was the first day of a new year and the rest of his and Kate's lives, to use the old cliché, and he wanted to celebrate that.

He knew from speaking to her via webcam that, with a month to go, she was feeling hugely pregnant and lethargic. The baby was lying large and low now, and she'd complained her ankles were swollen. He'd encouraged her to use today to rest and read.

Since the revelations of Christmas night, their relationship had become far tighter. When she looked at him now, he detected something shining in her eyes that made him feel on top of the world; it filled him with warmth, strength, and power. While he'd been away, he'd thought long and hard about what that meant to him. He felt proud and pleased that he seemed to have proved to her that he was a man of honor who was as good as his word—but that now presented him with a new problem. He knew he had it in himself to be a good husband, but could he find it in himself to say, "I love you"? He had shocked himself by realizing that he wanted to. But did he actually have the courage? The two women he'd loved the most had left him, and others had proved unworthy. His chest ached with a strange pressure as conflicting thoughts raced through his mind.

Midafternoon, he arrived home to find Kate lying on the sofa feeling restless. The book she was pretending to read wasn't holding her interest and the Yule log in the fireplace was just a small glowing lump of bark and ember now. He bent to massage her shoulders and kiss the top of her head."

"Hey, *agape mou*, how are you feeling?"

She sighed. "I'm a bit stir-crazy, staying confined to the villa. And I've got a headache. I'd love to get out for a bit." She looked toward the picture window. Outside the sky had darkened, and there was a fine mist of drizzle on the glass. The waves crashed as they hit the beach below, and even the normally tranquil infinity pool was gray and rippling. "I wanted to go down and walk on the beach, but I decided that making my way down the steep cliff path wasn't a good idea now that I resemble a beachball."

Aleksei laughed. "You don't look like a beachball, you look beautiful." He was being truthful—she looked ripe and gorgeous. "If you'd like, we could drive out to Sophia's Bay and just sit in the car for a short while. It will be wild weatherwise, but some fresh air and the different surroundings might just buck you up. I'll get you home in time for you to get bathed and changed for tonight's festivities."

She was already wearing a heavy cotton smock top over a T-shirt and jeans with a stretchy waistband, so he urged her to put on another heavier woolen sweater and change into warmer socks and her boots. He grabbed his coat, car and front door keys, and went along to the kitchen to wave them at Hestia to demonstrate they were going out. The housekeeper looked a little concerned but said nothing.

The coastal road was being buffeted by gusts of wind as they drove along to Sophia's Bay. Kate had perked up now and was chattering nineteen to the dozen. He listened raptly, loving how her beautiful face was filled with vibrancy and animation.

When they got to the Point, he parked the car and wondered if they should turn around immediately and go home: the windshield was lashed by squalling rain and the gale made a howling sound around the vehicle. Even though it was a four-wheel drive, he could the car shaking against the pounding of the wind. Out at sea, he could see dark rolling clouds and flashes of lightning. The dramatic and spectacular view was exhilarating and stimulating. He could sense that Kate felt instantly enlivened.

He watched as she leaned her arms on the console and supported her chin with her hands. He remembered that his mother and his twin, Andreas, had lost their lives in a similar kind of storm at Aphrodite's Point. That particular thought used to send a chill down his spine, but now, here, it affected him less. Was that because he was here with Kate, that he knew he had her love?

"Perhaps we should go back now," Kate said suddenly. "This place is decidedly eerie in this kind of weather."

He was just about to agree with her, because he didn't want her getting tired, when he spotted a small figure in a green anorak hunched up almost in a ball in the shelter of one of the caves in the side of the sandstone cliff down in the bay. The person's head appeared to be hanging down in its despairing hands.

Kate spotted the figure, too, and pointed. She wiped some condensation from the windshield and then exclaimed, "*Eleni.*"

Aleksei realized she was right. "What the hell?" He scrambled out of the car and walked a few steps, then peered through the mist and lashing rods of rain. He called out, though he wasn't sure that Eleni could hear him above the noise of the waves and the storm. But something must have caught the girl's eye, because she looked up. For long moments, she just stared as he waved his hands and made gestures for her to come back onto the beach; it was clear that the tide was coming in and soon she would be stranded. Then she seemed to realize her impending predicament and scrambled to her feet, picking her way over the rocks to where Aleksei stood, her arms hugged around herself against the wind.

As Eleni approached, he could see that her small pointed face was blotchy and streaked with weeping.

"Eleni, whatever is the matter?"

The girl stopped and stood awkwardly, wiping her face with her anorak sleeve and kicking pebbles out of the sand. Then her face puckered, and she started crying again.

"Hey." He took a step forward and put her arms around her. His stepsister wept for a minute or so until her tears subsided a little.

"Why don't you come back to the car," he suggested soothingly. "Kate's waiting there. We can go home to the villa, get warm and dry, and I'll have Hestia make us hot chocolate, and you can tell us all about it."

Eleni gave a big sniff and nodded. Aleksei turned her and, an arm still around her shoulder, walked her back to the four-by-four. Just before they reached the vehicle, Eleni stopped and turned.

"I'm sorry, Aleksei, but…I…I'm so unhappy…" She started to cry again.

"What's the matter, *gliko mou*?" he said solicitously. "Can it really be that bad?"

"Y-es," the girl gulped. "Pavlos doesn't want to go out with me because he says I'm a crazy druggie."

"Pavlos?"

Eleni looked devastated, through her tears. "He's a guy I really like… He was at my friend's Christmas party the other night and he turned me down in front of everybody…"

"Eleni," Aleksei exclaimed, realizing he was sounding irritated. He made an effort to soften his tone. "The boy's an idiot. Everyone knows that you're doing really well now."

"No, they don't," Eleni gabbled. "All the people at the party, they started laughing at me, and Demetria Niarchos said that no guy would ever want to go out with me now that I've been in rehab—"

Aleksei made to give her a comforting squeeze, but Eleni gave a howl, threw off his arm, and then turned and started running toward the next bay where Aphrodite's Point lay.

At that moment, Kate came to his side, her long auburn hair whipping and tangling in the fierce wind.

"Kate—get back into the car. It's too rough for you out here."

"What's the matter with her, Aleksei?"

"Oh, she's upset. Some boy's rejected her publicly because of her substance abuse, and now she's run off—"

He was surprised when Kate interjected vehemently, "You've got to go after her, she'll be distraught. That sort of humiliation at that age can be devastating." Tears were flowing freely down her face, and not just because of the wind. "Aleksei, please, she could do something silly." She grabbed his arm as she urged him.

A chord struck within him: Kate was speaking from experience. She knew what it was to be a teenager and to be taken down like that in front of a crowd. And Eleni was already so vulnerable...

"Okay, I'll go get her and try again to persuade her to come home with us. But only if you go back to the car now," he ordered.

"All right," Kate agreed. "But hurry. The tide's almost in."

Aleksei let a long breath, then turned and went toward the cliff's edge. He saw that Eleni had made it down to the causeway and was starting out across the pavement, even though the tide had begun to partly obscure it.

"Eleni—stop," he called, cupping his hands to his mouth in the hope that the sound of his warning would carry. But

Eleni kept on running toward Aphrodite's little temple perched out on its rock, the water splashing up to her knees now.

"Eleni." It was no good. For helpless seconds, Aleksei stood and just watched as Eleni scrambled at the foot of the island, then his insides lurched with horror as he heard a cry and the distant figure slipped and fell down into the turbulent water.

"Oh my God." Without thinking, he started down the hill to the beach, keeping his eyes firmly on Eleni, who appeared to have passed out and was lying facedown in the rising sea. He set out across the causeway as fast as he dared. The pavement was obscured now because the tide was coming in fast, and as he got nearer to the Point, he was nearly thigh-deep in water, which slowed him down. A little farther on, a wave smashed against him and he almost lost his balance entirely. But years of daily workouts stood him in good stead and he steadied himself and resumed pushing against the barrier of the sea in order to reach his stepsister. Thankfully, the rough waves had pushed her onto the rocks, but as he got very near, Aleksei could see she was barely conscious and there was a nasty gash on her cheek, pouring blood down her white face.

Finally he got to her and hauled her out of the water and up on to the small island and into the safety of the temple. Gasping for breath, he rubbed her hands and face as he tried to revive her. It struck him that she could have inhaled seawater, so with some difficulty, he repositioned her and attempted resuscitation.

"Come on, Eleni, come on," he yelled, massaging her chest. Suddenly the girl made a choking sound, and he swiftly moved her into the recovery position just as she vomited.

As the waves crashed around them, the wind screeched and howled in and out of the temple columns and the low rumble of thunder came overhead, he fumbled in the inside pocket where his phone was stowed. It was getting really dark now, and the rain was torrential. Thankfully, the phone was dry, but try as he might he couldn't get a signal and call for help. Damn. He looked up at the cliff top. He couldn't see Kate. She must be safely back in the car. He hoped to God that she would realize he and Eleni were in trouble and use the Bluetooth to raise the alarm.

The ground was slippery, and Kate had to curb her speed as she made her way back to the car. It was so difficult to walk against the wind, given her size. She was out of breath, and the lashing rain had soaked her jeans and boots. Inches from the vehicle, she felt her feet go out from under her, and she slipped and fell heavily, and without dignity, on her bottom. She felt a slash of pain around her lower spine, and the air was knocked out of her lungs. She moved her arms to support her tummy protectively. She attempted to haul herself back up but failed. She could feel the baby wriggling around in her womb, and her lower back really hurt.

She wasn't sure how long she sat there. She was aware of how drenched and cold she was and also of how her strength was ebbing away. She could also feel a low, dull but insistent pain spreading in her lower abdomen and then something warm spreading across the crotch and legs of her pants. The lower half of her body was suddenly consumed by a rush of extreme pain, and then another, but she couldn't move her legs. She just wanted to lie down. She was tired, so very tired...

After a while, she heard voices—male voices—and was vaguely aware of being pulled and lifted, which really hurt. She knew that she was groaning loudly... Where was Aleksei? She wanted to tell him that she loved him, but she couldn't find strength to speak...

Chapter Sixteen

Kate became conscious that she was warm and dry. She realized she was lying in a hospital bed, hooked up to two drips—pain relief and a monitor, which beeped hurriedly. Those agonizing contractions were coming regularly now. She turned her head and saw Aleksei next to her, leaning forward, his expression unusually anxious.

"The baby," she managed. "He's coming—"

"Hush, *agape mou*," Aleksei soothed, his hand griping hers. "The doctor has everything under control." He hesitated, then went on to explain gently, "He has to perform an emergency cesarean."

Kate made a sound of protest, but Aleksei squeezed her hand reassuringly. "You won't know a thing about it, and the baby will soon be delivered safely."

Kate found her voice again. "It's too soon," she cried.

"It's okay, sweetheart, it's okay."

At that point, two nurses came into the room. Aleksei

moved away from the bed and stood up. "They're here to take you to the operating room," he informed her softly. He bent down to kiss her slowly and tenderly on the temple, his lips trailing to her ear, as she thought she heard him whisper, "I love you…"

Aleksei chose to wait outside the delivery room, his head bent onto his clenched fists. Inside, the lives of his wife and his son hung in the balance; Kate had lost a lot of blood after she'd fallen. His eyes were fogged with moisture as his own life played before him like a drowning man's. He hadn't had the best of childhoods, and his first marriage had been a costly, painful disaster. But his subsequent behavior—bedding and discarding women, treating them like toys—had he earned himself some kind of karma or cosmic retribution? He offered up a prayer, made a bargain: he would repent, do anything, if Kate and their baby were saved. He loved her.

A gentle hand touched his shoulder, and he looked up, the tears streaming down his face now, and saw Dafnia. He tried wiping his face with his palm, but he couldn't stop the flood.

"I don't know what I'll do if I lose them, *Thia*," he said, his voice small and thick with emotion. "I love Kate so much."

"Hush, *agori mou*." She eased herself down beside him with the help of her cane. "You know, this is the first time I've seen you cry since you were a very, very small boy. When your dear mother and brother died, you didn't cry then, or ever afterward. I truly believed that your heart turned to stone that day. But it seems that you have finally let love back into your life and your heart."

"But what if they die, *Thia*? I can't go on without her."

"We must trust that the gods are with us, *agori mou*. And if Kate and the baby come through this safely, you know what you must do…"

When Kate came around after the operation, she felt groggy and very sore. When she tried to sit up, she couldn't, as she was still hooked up to a couple of drips, and the nurse who had been assigned to her leaped up to coax her back into lying down. Then the woman went to a phone mounted on the wall and made a call in Greek that Kate mostly couldn't understand. Within minutes, Aleksei was at her bedside, smiling broadly.

"What happened to the baby," Kate pleaded weakly. "Where is he? Is he all right?"

"He's beautiful," Aleksei replied proudly. "He's doing well." He reached out to run the back of his hand down her cheek. "You've done so well, too. He's a good weight, considering he's arrived a little early. He's going to be hooked up to a cardiorespiratory monitor for the next few hours because his lungs may be a little immature, and he's also receiving intravenous fluids. I have requested that Dr. Leandros, the specialist, fly in from Athens as soon as the weather improves. But the local obstetrician here is optimistic that he will catch up very quickly."

"Oh, thank God," Kate breathed, relief flooding through her.

"He's a fine, healthy boy, *agape mou*. If he had gone to full term, I think you would have had a hard time giving birth."

Kate smiled wanly, though inside her heart leaped with joy. "When can I see him?"

"Soon. But you need to rest after the procedure. You've lost a lot of blood, and you are very weak. Later, the doctor wants to give you the chance to try and feed him yourself. The nurses are going to arrange for you to be taken to the neonatal unit when you've had a chance to recover some of your strength."

"How is Eleni?" Kate asked, her voice full of concern and suddenly feeling agitated because she had no memory of the girl being rescued.

"She's doing okay, too," Aleksei assured her, a shadow passing over his features. "She has a nasty cut on her cheek, which required minor surgery, and she swallowed some seawater, so she is being checked out to make sure that she hasn't damaged her lungs. But she should be able to return home in a couple of days.

"If it hadn't been for Hestia raising the alarm because we were gone so long and she was worried that the weather was worsening, help might not have arrived in time for us. Thankfully the local police chief took her call seriously and started to search the area surrounding the villa for us. It was *Thia* Dafnia who suggested that Eleni might have gone down to Sophia's Bay."

She searched his face and saw that his eyes looked raw and watery. Had he been crying? "I'm so sorry," she whispered contritely, realizing just how much trouble she must have caused.

"Why are you sorry, *hriso mou*?" Aleksei placed his hand over hers, being careful not to dislodge the cannula. "You couldn't help what happened." He closed his eyes briefly. "Though I can't lie that it could have ended in tragedy." He opened his eyes again and smiled through tears. "Thank God, you and the baby are just fine."

"Don't cry, sweetheart," she urged him. "It's going to be okay."

They sat for a while in silence, his hand resting on hers. Then exhaustion and the remains of the anesthetic forced her to close her eyes, and within seconds she had fallen asleep.

When she awoke a couple of hours later, she saw Dafnia sitting quietly and patiently in the chair next to the bed. The older woman stirred and leaned across the bed to put a reassuring hand on Kate's shoulder. "How are you feeling, my dear?"

The kindness and concern in Dafnia's voice was too much for Kate, and she welled up.

"There, there. You are very tired and shocked. And I think you are wanting to see your baby, no?"

Kate nodded mutely.

"I understand that you will be taken to see him. You needed to get a little rest first. You mustn't worry. He's the most beautiful boy, and once you have been able to hold him and maybe to feed him, you will feel so much better." She squeezed Kate's shoulder. "Aleksei has barely left his side since he came into the world. I have never seen him so besotted," she mused.

"He wanted the baby more than anything in the world," Kate replied in a small voice.

"Besides you, that is, my dear," Dafnia added. "He adores you so much."

Kate felt startled by Dafnia's observation. She didn't know what to say.

Dafnia looked at her shrewdly and said, "You seem surprised by that, Kate." She fixed her with her wise brown gaze. "But believe me, Aleksei loves you so much. When he thought that he might have lost you, he was distraught. But it has been clear to the rest of the family since he introduced you to us that, for the first time in his life, Aleksei has found love. I know, I know—he doesn't always show it in ways that are easy to accept. Be patient with him. It is a new experience for him; he has never allowed such an emotion to be part of his life before. However, you have broken through and touched his heart. He is yours for life, if you will let him be."

At that, she gave Kate's shoulder a pat and stood up. "The family loves you, too, Kate. You have brought us wonderful gifts—you have given me my great-nephew and you helped save Eleni's life tonight. And," she added, "you have brought my nephew the happiness he deserves.

"Now, are you feeling well enough to go and see your little boy now? Good. I will get the nurse to take you down to him."

After Dafnia left the room, Kate lay staring at the ceiling, stunned. Dafnia's words went round and round in her head. *Aleksei loves you so much... Be patient with him... You have broken through and touched his heart.* Just as she had literally come to live in a foreign land in order to be his wife, emotionally he had done the same in becoming her husband. Perhaps Dafnia was right: he did love her, but just not in ways that she always recognized.

She recalled the times when he'd shown the utmost care for her and cherished her—and when he'd finally said, "I love you." Yes, he had. Just before she'd been taken down to theater for the baby's delivery…

A nurse arrived with a wheelchair, which she presumed was to take her along to the neonatal unit to see her son. As she was pushed along the corridor, still attached to the blood bag and another drip, she felt increasingly nervous. How would it feel to meet her son for the first time? Would she be able to hold him and feed him?

She noticed a clock on the wall. It stood at ten minutes to midnight. Of course: it was New Year's Eve.

The nurse guided her through double doors into a large room in which there were two small cribs surrounded by an army of machines. Her heart beat wildly in her chest. By one of the cribs stood her husband. Though his chinos were crumpled and had saltwater stains on them, his shirt was partly unbuttoned and its sleeves rolled up, and he looked dead tired, he was still the most gorgeous man in the universe. Then her heart nearly stopped beating altogether as she caught sight of the tiny bundle lying in the clear-sided cradle, swaddled tightly, his spiky dark hair sticking out from under a small white woolen cap. Her baby!

Aleksei turned and stared at her briefly. Kate registered the unfamiliar look of uncertainty in his eyes. The nurse parked the wheelchair near the crib and gestured to Aleksei to lift his son out of it. He bent down and with the utmost gentleness picked up the wriggling, swaddled mite, supporting the baby's little head with his large hand. Kate witnessed the pure love that suffused her husband's expression as he made soothing noises, and her throat became constricted by emotion.

Carefully Aleksei handed the child to Kate and stood back while the nurse helped her open her gown and try to tempt her son to take her breast. The tiny boy nuzzled and searched blindly at first, but then, with Kate's guidance, suddenly found her nipple and began sucking eagerly, his wee fists pummeling and grasping at her soft flesh. To begin with, it hurt a lot, but as the seconds went by and she could hear the satisfied baby grunts, Kate relaxed. She didn't think she had ever felt such an intense rush of love for anyone or anything.

She watched transfixed as her son fed, then raised her eyes to meet Aleksei's shining gaze as he watched also. The nurse, satisfied that all was well, discreetly left the room.

"Will you forgive me?" he asked softly.

"Why do I need to forgive you?" she replied, feigning a wide-eyed look.

"Because I have behaved like a selfish pig."

"Yes, there have been times when you have," she agreed with a rueful grin.

He raised an eyebrow at her pert reply.

She fixed him with a direct look. "But I love you just as you are…and I vow to tell you everything I'm thinking from now on, if you'll do the same."

He raised his other eyebrow and inclined his head. "Everything? Are you offering me some kind of new deal, Mrs. Aleksanou?"

"Those are my terms, Mr. Aleksanou. New year, new you, new me, new marriage."

"I think I can agree to that," he confirmed wryly, a slow smile tugging at his lips.

There was a silence as Aleksei surveyed her. Kate busied herself with repositioning the baby, who'd had his fill, and rearranging her gown.

"I love you very much," Aleksei said quietly.

"I know," Kate replied, looking up him, her eyes shining.

On Easter Saturday, a happy party of family and friends was gathered on the terrace of the Villa Aphrodite, basking in the warm spring sunshine, enjoying delicious food and champagne in celebration of the christening of Andreas Aleksanou, which had taken place at the church in Thira earlier in the day. The little boy was thriving now, and it was almost as if his premature entrance into the world had never happened.

Kate looked around at the party. Her mother was holding a gurgling Andreas in his lace christening gown and bonnet, while her father fussed around with his new camera and took pictures of the doting grandmother and her grandson. Dafnia stood close by, coming in to rearrange Andreas's gown and hat in between shots.

On the other side of the terrace, there was a table displaying all the generous gifts that had been given to Andreas and his proud parents—including a small silver spoon inscribed with the baby's date of birth from the staff at Aleksanou Associates in London—that was being examined by a happy Eleni and Pavlos, who had now become attached at the hip, it seemed. Eleni was doing so well. Pavlos visited her on New Year's Day in the hospital, and romance had blossomed after all. She'd also begun an apprenticeship, learning the craft of jewelry making at a studio in Thira, run by an expat German who had a sharp eye on the summer tourist trade, and she had made the most exquisite gold christening bracelet for Andreas as her first commission.

Hestia and Dimitri bustled among the other guests, bearing trays of canapés and drinks, while in another corner, Lydia—on a flying visit from London—talked animatedly to Marina and Adrastos about the fabulous new job that Aleksei had helped her land as temporary PA to a friend of his, wealthy Italian media magnate Luciano D'Angelo, who was launching the English edition of a weekly women's glossy in the British magazine market. Marina nodded animatedly, while Adrastos was bent, listening but keeping an eye on and offering a supporting hand to little ten-month-old Athena, who was trying hard to haul herself to her feet using her daddy's trouser leg.

Good old Lydia. She'd brought the latest edition of *Cool!* with her and had thrown open its pages at the start of an eight-page color spread that featured Phoenix Jones and her new fiancé, a megarich if slightly elderly and paunchy Russian oligarch called Boris.

"Blimey, look at size of the belly on him," Lydia had cackled.

"And look at the size of the rock on her," Kate had added wryly.

Aleksei had just sighed when she'd shown the magazine to him.

Aleksei...to say that he was a changed man would be a lie. He could still be the same infuriating, impossible but utterly irresistible man he'd always been. But one who, with a little prompting, talked to her now, checked her feelings, and even opened up about what he was really thinking. She found it easy to do the same. They were a team, a dream team, with a perfect, wonderful baby boy…

She jumped as Aleksei's arms snaked around her waist and his lips brushed the side of her neck.

"Everybody looks as though they are enjoying themselves," he murmured. "Do you think we could steal away for a few minutes on our own?"

"Oh, I think so," Kate replied. "I don't think they'll notice that we've gone missing."

As the guests continued chatting, laughing, eating, and drinking, Kate and Aleksei slipped past them and down the steps that led to the beach. A breeze tugged at the hem of Kate's cream and pale lemon silk dress and ruffled her hair. Gentle waves lapped at the sand as she took off her shoes and allowed Aleksei to lead her down to the water's edge.

He turned her to look at him and, cupping her face in his hands, kissed her, his tongue darting tantalizingly between her lips. Then he lifted his head and pulled her in close to him, resting his chin on her hair. She nestled into him, the salty smell of the sea mixing with the citrus scent of him.

"In six weeks' time, it'll be our first anniversary," Aleksei said.

Kate's head jerked up as she gazed at him, puzzled. "But our wedding anniversary isn't until the middle of August."

"I was thinking of the anniversary of our first time together."

"Ah." Kate's cheeks flushed at the memory, and she looked at him shyly from under her lashes. "I'm surprised that you remember it."

Aleksei smiled and ran his thumb tenderly across her cheek. "*Pethi mou*, it was a night never to be forgotten. And for that reason I think we should repeat it—but this time on an island in the Caribbean."

"The Caribbean? But we can't leave Andreas—"

Aleksei laid a silencing finger on her lips. "Andreas and his nanny will be coming with us. There are two small villas next door to each other on this private island. They will have one and we will have the other, so that we can recreate that amazing first night to our heart's content."

Kate colored up again. "As usual, you've thought of everything. Well, what can I say but yes?"

Aleksei gazed down at her, his lips twitching in another suppressed smile. "I think I have found myself a wonderful wife—one who is a truly a wife in *every* sense." And then he planted another lingering kiss on her lips before she could protest...

About the Author

Joanne Walsh got hooked on romance when her grandma gave her a copy of *Gone with the Wind*. The teachers at her strict girls' school didn't approve of a ten-year-old reading such a 'racy' novel and confiscated it. But Joanne still became a voracious romance reader and, later, an editor for one of the world's leading women's fiction publishers, where she could do two of her favorite things: work with her beloved alpha-male heroes and spend time in the USA.

These days, Joanne lives in the south of England and divides her time between freelance editing, writing and spending time with her very own real-life alpha, including riding pillion on his 2.3 Triumph Rocket motorcycle.

Printed in Great Britain
by Amazon